From the Author of

When Gucci Came First
(True Tales of a Tramp)

KJ Three Six Five (The Diary Vol. I)
4 Miles to Freedom
&
Man Unnecessary

WildChild Press Presents...

The follow up to the International Five Star Seller
WHEN GUCCI CAME FIRST

The 2nd installment of the Kalico Jones Trilogy

And to YOU, homeboy, I say "Thanks!"

By: Mia Williamson aka "Kalico Jones"

And to You, Homeboy, I say "Thanks!"
Written by: Mia Williamson
WildChild Press Montclair, NJ 07042

ISBN: 0-9753082-1-1

Although this book is based on real life situations and circumstances, its contents are fiction. This book contains strong language and is not intended for minors.

Any resemblance to any persons, places or things is purely coincidental and should be regarded as such

.

Written by: Mia R. Williamson
Known by these works as
"Kalico Jones"
January 2006

WildChild Press
Printed in U.S.A.

Dear Reader:

I would like to first begin with a "thank you." I've received so much love and support from you with my first novel, When Gucci Came First, and I want you to know that since then I have made a serious attempt at not only healing, but also moving on.

I have grown as a person and as a single parent, I am amazing. I can finally say I am good at something other than…
Although my first novel has isolated me from old friends and family, I can honestly say, those who really love me and truly matter are still around. People tend to get "caught up" in this book game, thinking they are going to strike it rich by telling some story about how much money they spent, drugs they sold, drugs they used, celebrities they fucked, etc. = the new "hip hop fiction" genre, but for me, writing is an outlet, a form of release, a form of relief, and ultimately, a way of moving on. By no means do I want to "big up" any of the people who helped me take advantage of myself.

It was told to me, "Pain is weakness leaving the body." I responded with, "Well I hope when the weakness leaves, it takes some of these extra pounds I've put on with it."

In this book I give you what is left of my old life and allow you to witness first hand, the transformation from that fragile young lady searching for someone to love her, to the grown ass me, who still makes mistakes, but takes full responsibility for her life. Knowing I am my own "difference maker" and no one else.

"May God grant you everything you ask for during your quiet time with Him."
KJ

My love for Two Brothers:

I want to publicly put you on a pedestal.

To let you know just how much you mean to me.

I remember meeting you and saying,

"I don't want to do this book thing anymore!"

In my heart, I was done.

But you said,

"Kal…you're not finished!"

And you said,

"So you're the Infamous Kalico Jones!"

And although our lives are not the same as they were the day we met

You guys with your BIG businesses

and me with my projects

Our meeting although by chance

is one I will NEVER forget

I appreciate your honesty.

despite one of you being more "brutal" in his expression than the

other

but I applaud you …the both of YOU.

I love you BOTH forever.

xoxoxo

From Kool Kal to the ONES who got away!

(Each time I speak with these Brothers they always encourage me to do
my best. That's why they are forever "GOOD money" to me.)

In loving Memory of The man who said, "Just make sure your daughter can spell her name before she learns how to do the Butterfly (dance)," Tootie (William G.) Mt. Vernon, NY - You will never be forgotten R.I.P.

To my daughter, Ivana
You were truly meant to be

So nice, I have to say this twice...
This book is fiction! I know with When Gucci Came First, many of
you thought the contents of that book were real. When its contents
were truth based, but fiction nonetheless. Please do not take the
contents of this book out of context. This book should be considered as a means of entertainment only, as it was written to entertain
you, the reader.

**Resemblance to any person(s), place(s) or thing(s) is purely co-
incidental and should be regarded as such**
a.k.a "The disclaimer."

And to YOU, Homeboy, I say
"Thanks!"

And to YOU, Homeboy, I say "Thanks!"

And here is the continuation of "MY" story. Me, Kalico Jones, author and mother of one. Sexually abused, physically abused, cocaine addiction, cigarettes and now I'm stuck with a drinking problem. I'm a fighter though and I know things are going to be much better for me in the year to come.

So what about me?

Well I write this book about my life – When Gucci Came First – and it's a showstopper. People actually stop me on the street, they write me letters, they are in love with Kalico Jones. I reveal things about myself most people would take to their grave.

After I kick the drug habit, open all my emotional baggage in public, and face the truth about my life and life in general, here comes a new kind of hurdle. I'm in a fragile place in life and if you read my first book, you know exactly what I mean.

Off to my story...

And to YOU, Homeboy, I say "Thanks!"

PRELUDE TO A REVELATION

Thanksgiving 2002

I think I'll check my cell phone messages before we head out. Good only one message…

"Hey Kalico this is LaToya, call me on my cell phone when you get this message."

What's up with HER calling me? I haven't heard from THEM since the break up between me and her brother (homeboy). I called her back and passed the phone to my daughter, her niece.

"Say Happy Thanksgiving to your Aunt."

"Hi Auntie…here mommy I don't want it" and Ivy passed the phone back to me.

"So what's up?"

"Nothing, I'm up here at my brother's house for Thanksgiving."

"Really, that's nice."

"Kalico, he's hurting, he really wants to see his daughter."

"Really?"

"Yeah, I mean he IS paying child support and he misses his daughter."

And to YOU, Homeboy, I say "Thanks!"

"Oh well, he should have thought about that before he took me through all the drama."

"I know, I know, but she is his daughter."

"Yeah and…" I sucked my teeth.

Now I know this bitch didn't call me on Thanksgiving for this! Last Thanksgiving her brother was at my house fixing breakfast for me and his daughter, lying his ass off about how…fuck it, that ain't the issue.

Anyway, LaToya was calling me to tell me how her brother was so hurt and how he needed to see his daughter.

Hmmmm I think I'll entertain this conversation, but only for five minutes 'cause I have to be on Roosevelt Island at my Aunt's house by five for the family dinner.

"Kalico, my brother wants to be a good father and he *was* a good father before all this stuff happened, I told him y'all were moving and he is hurt." Damn, her vocabulary is limited! (hurt, hurt, hurt).

"I don't know how your brother sleeps at night, knowing that he is a dead beat Dad and I mean the kind of dead beat that GOES BEYOND child support, I ain't even talking about the child support."

"He can't sleep, he's a mess," she continued.

Okay, I've heard just about enough of this bullshit! wanted to cuss her ass out. She's been on the phone with me about four minutes and not once did she address all the shit I'VE been through for

And to YOU, Homeboy, I say "Thanks!"

the past year and change at the hands of her brother. I mean, she IS a single parent, and doing very well at it, so she of all people should know that raising a child alone is DO-ABLE, right? Wrong... 'cause all she kept talking about was how hurt his black ass was. He's hurting...he can't sleep...he misses his daughter, fuck him! He should have thought about that before he took my daughter to that bitch's house. He should have thought about that when his ass was fuckin' with that old lady he met in a bar DURING our relationship, who might I add, lived around the corner from me with FIVE, count 'em FIVE mother fucking kids and all the while he was staying over there, he NEVER ONCE stopped to see his daughter on his way TO or FROM the old lady's house. He NEVER ONCE showed up at the hospital during the three plus weeks his daughter was in and out of the emergency room with clinical pneumonia. He NEVER ONCE sent a Christmas or Birthday card to his daughter, a daughter of whom as I write this sentence has only seen her father about eight times since I had to move us up out of that condo in Spring Valley.

And by the way and come to think of it...NO ONE in his family has ever sent a card to my daughter or even acknowledged her since the break up. And now, almost two years to the fuckin' day I left his ass, his sister calls me with the "he's hurting" shit.

She CAN'T be fuckin' serious!

He's hurting and wants to see his daughter, (I'm exhaling), he should have thought about that before he hooked up with this new bitch! Oops, I mean this NEW "young lady"...NEW (I'm sucking my teeth) only to MY knowledge, because from what I hear, they've been together for over a year now.

Who's the young lady? Well she's the one I had an order of protection against for the entire three years of our relationship. She's the one who my dear EX called the police on after she attempted to fight me during my pregnancy. SHE'S the young lady who tried to fix my dear EX up with her best friend during our relationship, so they could double date, since she was fuckin' his man, Mr. BMW. She's also the same one who went to the police and falsely accused me of harassment, had me thrown in jail not once, but TWICE! I had two warrants for my arrest and had to post bail. But that's not even all of it…In June of 1997 she attempted to assist THREE other young women in "jumping" me outside of the projects on 141st and Seventh avenue in Harlem. She's the young lady of whom my dear EX said he wasn't even fuckin' with to not only me, but to everyone else. Who is she? She's the one he loves now and rightfully so…I mean they do live together.

What a fuckin' joke!
Now back to the telephone call…

"Listen LaToya, your brother has lied…he has allowed his girlfriend to falsely accuse me of things to the police, I lost a 58,000 dollar a year job because I was sitting in jail facing felony charges when I should have been sitting in a Manager's meeting…and instead of her coming to court to face me, she just kept not showing up until the charges were dropped...and not ONCE during this time, did your brother call his daughter, write his daughter or even acknowledge her birthday and I STILL sent him father's day cards and pictures and stuff for his birthday from his daughter. Fuck him!"

"Don't say that, he's hurting and again...he IS paying his child support"

"Yeah, and he better KEEP paying if his ass doesn't want to go to jail. Listen (taking a deep breath), I don't feel sorry for your brother and why in the hell should I? He assaulted me in the street in front of our daughter and my cousin, he tried to sue me for custody and brought the girlfriend's sister with him to court, who politely stood up and said that your brother had paternity concerns regarding our daughter. And then he topped off her behavior by adding (and this is a quote), 'but my name isn't even on the little girl's birth certificate!'...y'all must be crazy. If he loves this young lady, that's okay. I can't knock love, and it's not for me to judge where a person finds love, but my daughter is NOT going to her house, my daughter is NOT going to be in her presence and that's that. She's done too many things to hurt my daughter and so that is NOT going to happen. And as far as your brother wanting to see his daughter, he should have shown up when the courts granted him visitation, he fucked that up all by himself."

"But Kalico, he really loves her (talking about the girl and NOT his daughter)."

"Then he should marry her, because that's the only way my daughter is ever going to be around her ass and that will have to be court ordered! He should be more concerned with...you know what, I'm not even going to go there. Just let your brother know that his license is going to be suspended for being almost 12,000 dollars in arrears and if he is stopped, he will be arrested for Criminal Non-Support, a felony in New York State."

"Well, call me back after nine, so my brother can talk to his daughter, my daytime minutes are low." She hung up.

I never did call her back.

(screaming loudly and running through my house)

"Yolanda!...Yolanda!" Yolanda is my friend a.k.a Long Distance "sister"- she and her daughter Brittney flew in from Atlanta to spend Thanksgiving with me and my family. She's been one of the reasons I've been able to focus lately.

"What's up girl?"

"Throw out all the Champagne, throw out all the liquor...there will be no more drinking for me and no more late night cigarettes!"

"Why, what happened?"

"I just got off the phone with Homeboy's (my dear EX's) sister and after that conversation, my biggest fear is dying and Ivy ends up having to live with him!"

I only drink on very special occasions.

And I owe it all to Homeboy... "Thanks Homeboy!"

And to YOU, Homeboy, I say "Thanks!"

Reflections

I must admit my current circumstance is largely due to my
inability to let go of a useless situation.
My inability to cut the cord (so to speak),
when it comes to holding on to hope.
Hope for what?
Hope for something that may never be
Something for my daughter...
a father

And to YOU, Homeboy, I say "Thanks!"

I can't believe I'm stuck here, in the house, with a baby, while HIS ass is out running the streets. I have no money, no food and I'm all the way in Spring Valley. I called my friend Monet. She left her job and came right over, handed me $100.00 (of which I haven't paid her back to this date) and proceeded to give me the advice that every woman in my situation gets from that one girlfriend, who even though you are down in the dumps, feels she has to give you in order to **KEEP IT REAL...**

"Girl you need to leave his ass! This shit is crazy, in the house with a newborn and no money, he can't be serious!" she continued... "Where's the food? Where's the pampers?"

That's when it HIT me, my ass needed to put together that FUCK YOU money quick. I had to not only exit, but exit with a kid. Where did this go wrong? I checked the time; it was 1 O'clock in the afternoon, is he okay? And if he is okay, where is he? The phone rang.

Ring...ring...
"Hello" (it was a famous R&B singer)
"Yo what up Kalico, yo "Wiz" (short for Wisdom), just left my house, he's on his way home, aight?"
I said okay and hung up the phone, but I was on fire. How DARE Mr. Famous R&B Singer call my house to tell me that MY MAN was on his way home at 1 O'clock in the afternoon. Where in the

     The 2nd Installment of the Kalico Jones Trilogy

hell was he all night? I put the baby in her crib and waited for him to open the door. It's now 2:30pm and homeboy is just walking in the house, he's drunk and shit...looking pitiful, talking about, "I know...I know...I fucked up, I'm sorry...you mad?"

I took a deep breath, no this nigga did not just ask me if I was mad, he must have bumped his fucking head on the way upstairs. I closed my eyes and thought to myself...I should slap his ass but he's so drunk he probably wouldn't feel it. I will be calm...I will not hit him...I will just
leave...I will be calm...I will not hit him...I will just leave...I will be calm...I will not hit him...I will just leave. I looked at him and in a damn near whisper said, "Yes, I am mad, I'm furious, you're a father now, we are a family, this is crazy...I'm leaving!"
Two weeks later I was gone!

Leaving was the best thing I could have done for me and my daughter. Since the move, I have published three books, excuse me I mean four, my daughter is also an author, we've started great careers for ourselves and my daughter is stress free. Where is homeboy? I don't know exactly, but by the looks of the Special Edition SUV, I would assume he's doing just fine.

Just fine...(taking a deep breath) that's hard to believe, as I never would have thought I would be in this position – raising a child by myself, with no emotional support from him at all. It's puzzling to

And to YOU, Homeboy, I say "Thanks!"

me, especially when I look back on how great our relationship was
in the beginning.
And in the beginning...was the word and the word was...

And to YOU, Homeboy, I say "Thanks!"

INTRODUCTION
SUMMER 1999 HARTLEY PARK, MT. VERNON – NY

"Yo Kalico, this guy Wisdom wants to meet you, he's over there in the burgundy Lexus."

It was my friend, Azure trying to introduce me to this high yellow light skinned man with gold teeth. I looked at Azure and said, "Girl now you know I can't get with a nigga with gold teeth."

"But he's driving a Lexus, he works hard for a living and he's offering to take us to City Island for dinner tonight, just say hello so we can go get some seafood," Azure pleaded.

"I don't care how hard he works, he's high yellow and has gold teeth in his mouth! And yeah the car is nice, but I'm just not into that anymore."

"Yeah right" Azure snickered, "Once a ho…always a ho."

Boy oh boy did she not know what I've been through. And how could she? I haven't lived in Mt. Vernon with any regularity in about seven years. I walked to the store. Mr. Burgundy Lexus got out of his car and walked over to this lady with blonde twists in her hair, who I later found out was a relative of his.

And to YOU, Homeboy, I say "Thanks!"

The BOTH watched me walk to the store.

"Hello"

"Hey," I responded.

It was Mr. Burgundy Lexus trying to introduce himself to me, with Azure looking on in what seemed like disappointment. She quickly walked over, "Kalico this is Wisdom, Wisdom this is Kalico, now exchange numbers so we can meet up later for some food and drinks."

I laughed. Azure reminded me so much of myself when I was her age that it was scary. She was hated by many and loved by few, but the few who loved her, had her back. Just like me I tell you and had the sweetest heart in the world. Azure would give you her last if you needed it. She was just like that and her and Gary made a cute couple.

And Gary and Wisdom were friends. Which made our association "normal" as far as the public was concerned.

And to YOU, Homeboy, I say "Thanks!"

OUR FIRST DATE

Ring…ring… ring…

I looked down at my cell phone. I didn't recognize the number so I let it go to voice mail.

"This is Wisdom…ummm, I'm tired of calling you. If you don't call me back, I will take it as though you do not want to go out with me…ummm I'm not calling you again."

Damn! Has it been two weeks already? You see since I had touched down in Mt. Vernon, I had been out every night. I was working for a major accounting firm in the World Financial Center and had been late just about everyday since I moved back. I knew my job was in jeopardy, but I didn't care. Every day late for work, because every night I was hanging out to the wee hours of the morning, drinking and shit.

I didn't think I was ready to settle down, but I knew I wanted to try to date someone seriously. I was embarking upon my 28th birthday and felt that it was the perfect time to start exercising my options as far as decent men were concerned. And for once, I didn't want someone to take care of me. I wanted a hard working man. Someone who knew the "streets" just as much as I did, who had no children and therefore no "ties" to anyone. **Translation: NO GIRLFRIEND AND NO CRAZY ASS BABY MOMMAS.**

I had enough of that in my past life.

I called Wisdom back. He picked up on the first ring, "Ooooh picking up on the first ring, who were you expecting?" I chuckled.
"Who's this?"
"This is Kalico, what's up?"
"Nothing, about to go wash my car"
"Really…I wanna come, the hoopty could use a wash."
"Well I'll be at the car wash on Columbus Avenue next to the diner, be there in twenty minutes."
"Okay, I'm on my way." I put on a pair of gray sweatpants and a black halter top – no bra of course and slipped into my DKNY sneakers for what would be the best first date of my life. I drove up and got out of my Nissan Sentra (one of my parting gifts from Mr. Orgasm – refer to book one) and walked over to him.

Damn, he was a cutie. He wore a t-shirt with the sleeves cut off (a shirt of which I still own to this day) and looked good in it. Nice body, beautiful tan complexion, white teeth and the two gold teeth suddenly didn't bother me. looked him up and down and then I made eye contact with my "friend" and said, "So… you weren't going to call me anymore."

"Nope, if you're too busy to call me back then you're too busy for me."

"I hear that, so what's up….Azure told me that you manage the Home Depot on Baychester for a living."

"Damn, what else did she tell you?"

"Nothing really, she just said you were a very nice guy."

Smiling he said, "You look good, everyone is staring at you."

"I know, that happens a lot."

He opened the trunk of his Lexus, pulled out two Heinekens from a cooler and gave one to me. He walked around me with a smirk on his face and said, "So YOU'RE Kalico?"

"Yeah, and whatever you've heard is probably not true or grossly exaggerated. People in this town tend to do that when it comes to me."

"Where did the scratches come from?" "Oh these (pointing to my breast area)…these are my welcome back to New York presents from Kelly, Bunny and the rest of the Holly Farms Crew."

He responded, "Jealousy is something else."

"Sure is, but I can handle it."

"So where are you from Miss Kalico?"

"Here, Mt. Vernon, but my travels had me in Jersey and a few other places. I haven't lived here in almost seven years. I decided to come back after my grandmother died. (Taking a deep breath) That was the plan before she died. For me to come back, live with her and find an apartment. But before I could do that, she passed away. I live with my father now."

"Oh"

"Yeah, which is more like me having my own apartment, because he's on the road six days a week."

"That's nice."

"Yeah, it is," I responded (staring at his well developed arms and chest). I regrouped and continued, "So what about you…where are you from? I've never seen you before, and I know everybody."

"Well I'm from Mt. Vernon, but like you haven't lived here in a while, actually I just came home."

"Really, from where?" Looking kind of shy he said, "I'll tell you about that another time."

We continued to wash the cars. And it was going well…well until he turned the hose on me. I was drenched. I then turned the hose on him. We were laughing and playing and yelling for each other to stop and then the water cut off. I took that as an opportunity to grab him and pull him close to me, I wanted to feel his arms around me. My heart was beating so fast, I think I was almost afraid. He leaned toward me… put his arms around my waist and whispered in my ear, "Is this what you want?" Damn, such a sexy voice. I put my hand on the back of his neck, leaned toward him and whispered back, "No… but I'll take it for now." We both started laughing. I inhaled his smell, and closed my eyes…damn the brother even smells sexy.

I backed up and he did too. I wanted to kiss him and get it out of the

And to YOU, Homeboy, I say "Thanks!"

way, as the hug did "something" to me. I was actually attracted to someone who was NOT putting hundred dollar bills down my shirt. Who would have thought?

I got in my car soaked to the bone, but since I had a great time, it didn't even bother me. I drove home. He followed.
He opened my car door, "Ok, so you're home safe, I will pick you up at eight, we can watch movies and have dinner at my house…that is if you want to."
"Sounds like a plan, but don't pick me up, I'll come to you."

When Wisdom left, I took a quick shower and got myself together. I was excited about having a real date and I looked forward to having a normal life. And normal it would be…even if it killed me. I was tired of people talking about me. And most of all, I was tired of giving people shit to talk about. This is why Wisdom and I decided to keep our association a secret.

My cell phone was ringing.
Ring…ring…ring…
Ring…ring…
"Hello" "Bitch, where are you?" It was Azure.
"Chillin' why what's up?"
"Come out with me, let's go downtown (Harlem)."
I put on my tired voice, "Girl, no can do, I'm in the bed." LYING I was actually sitting on the sofa eating the seafood spaghetti my new

friend cooked up for us. Wisdom put his ear to my cell phone. He could hear Azure's voice. He stared making faces and laughing. I started laughing too. I guess that's what pissed her off.

"Oh fuck you, Kalico…go ahead with your secret squirrel ass, I'll call you tomorrow." She hung up. Just then Wiz looks at me and says, "Where did you park your car?"
"Two blocks down and around the corner, she'll never find it if she does drive around here."

TWO BLOCKS DOWN
AND AROUND THE CORNER?

Because Wisdom lived on a busy street in Mt. Vernon and the LAST thing we wanted was for people to see us together. Why? Because we wanted to make sure WE wanted to be together first, that's why!

And besides that, Mt. Vernon is very small and everyone is in everyone ELSE'S business. And so for almost three months, I would park my car down by the Sugar Bowl (diner) on Fifth Avenue and Sanford Boulevard. Until...

Jumping up out of my sleep, shaking Wisdom, "Wake up, get up... what time is it?"

"It's a quarter to eleven, why?"

"Shit, I gotta be in Church at eleven, my father is giving a special sermon and he wants me to be there." I crawled out of bed, grabbed my skirt, "Damn, I'm not even gonna have enough time to go home and get dressed...give me a shirt to wear."

"What kind?"

"Any kind that will go with this skirt...give me a black shirt."

I grabbed a towel and washcloth and ran to the bathroom to take a shower. Yelling from the bathroom into the bedroom where Wisdom was, "My father is going to kill me if I ain't there on time, you gotta drive me to my car."

"Okay, well hurry up."

I jumped back into the tight beige skirt with the two splits from the night before and slipped on one of homeboy's shirts. Damn I know it is too hot for this shirt, and this is definitely NOT a church skirt. I'll sit in the back row. We left his apartment.

I looked both ways and made a run for it. It was bright as hell outside, but it was Sunday and before noon, so hopefully no one will see us. I got in his car. I looked at him. He didn't look the same as he did during our walk down the steps, something was wrong. Just then this girl comes over and directs a question to him…"What are you doing?" and without giving her eye contact he replied, "I'm taking my peoples to church, why?"

Pointing at me, she continued, "What is SHE doing in your car?"

"He's taking me to my Father's church, why?" I responded.

She sucked her teeth and walked away.

Now I usually don't get involved when niggas are handling their business, but she did ask about me and so since I was there, I figured…I may as well answer.

He pulled off.

"What was that all about? I know her, I used to hang out with her

mother and aunts, and I've never seen her act like that, what's up?"
"Nothing, she's just somebody I fucked with in the past."

I didn't say shit because it wasn't my problem and therefore it wasn't
my issue. I let him drive me to the church and gave him a kiss. "I'll
see you later."
"Kalico, are you cooking tonight or am I?"
I smiled and said, "We can cook together."
He pulled off. I knew he was going to have a rough morning.

JUST ANOTHER DAY...LIVING IN THE HOOD JUST ANOTHER DAY AROUND THE WAY

Rough morning why? Because when I left Mt. Misery....ooops excuse me, Mt. Vernon...people were still on that Kalico's a ho, Kalico's a coke head shit and so therefore he was going to hear everything a person could tell him about me and my past. I decided that since I really liked him, I would tell him everything there was to know about me before anyone else could tell him everything they THOUGHT they knew about me.

My father's sermon was great. It revolved around being Godly. My father sure can preach. I was proud. And although I was late, he was really happy to see me there supporting him – with the tight skirt on and all, sitting in the back row. Ha ha ha. My father. He didn't even care about my attire, he was just so proud of himself, introducing me to everyone. We have a great relationship.

So during the sermon I figured out how I would explain my past to Wisdom. I wanted to keep it REAL and so I was just going to tell him right? That was the plan until I met up with him later on that afternoon...

And to YOU, Homeboy, I say "Thanks!"

He got out of his car and said, "Is it true you slept with your best friend's father?"

Oh God, where did he get that story from? Okay, now is the time to explain that whole Kelly thing, "Kelly and I were best friends for a few years, until someone I was close to told her that I was sleeping with her father. I never slept with Kelly's father **(Lying)**. Her father and I did, however have a relationship. The nature of the relationship, I can't go into, but I will tell you this. If I had slept with Kelly's father, do you think she and I would have continued our friendship?"

"So why are y'all not speaking now?"

"Because Kelly set my friend Hev up to get robbed and he ended up getting shot because he did not give up his safe and jewelry. Hev told me to tell people he was dead and so I did. At the time I agreed to put it in the streets, I didn't know Kelly had something to do with what happened. And why would I? I mean aside from her going to jail for a minor forgery offense a few years back, and that whole credit card thing, I thought she was living her life on the straight and narrow."

Damn her life was a mess.

Okay but this is not about her – again, this is about me and so I will say this, I couldn't believe someone actually tried to tell him some shit about me.

"So who told you that, was it your ex, Roxanne? (the one who approached him while I was in the car)."

"Yeah AND she said you were a coke head."

"Well she should know, I was getting high with people in her family. So she's right on that, yes, I used to get high."

"Are you still getting high?"

"No"

"Since when?"

"Since I met you." He smiled. I think he thought I was gaming him, but I wasn't. I really was trying to change. I had made up my mind that in order for me to find someone to be with me, I had to clean myself up. So I stopped getting high. That's it, just stopped.

I grabbed his hand, looked him right in the eyes and said, "Listen, I'm not going to front like I'm some homebody chick who never ventured out or act like my reputation is not deserved, I'm just saying that I really like you and I want to be with you and whatever you need to know…just ask, I wont lie."

"I really like you too."

"Good, now what's for dinner?"

"Seafood"

We got in his car and drove to Pathmark.

And to YOU, Homeboy, I say "Thanks!"

THE STREETS

Ever since the news of me and homeboy's relationship had been made public, courtesy of his ex-girlfriend, each day I found myself explaining one rumor after another. Day in and day out, I was a "coke head" I was "a whore" I "fucked my best friend's father" It was crazy and then the ultimate… Homeboy walks in the door after a long day of work…"Kalico come in here, we need to talk."

I was in the kitchen cooking. "One sec, I'll be right there," I responded. I turned the flame down under the pot of rice and walked

into the bedroom. I could tell something was wrong by the look on his face. "What's up Baby?"

"Sit down" I sat down on the edge of his bed and thought to myself, "Damn this must be serious."

He took a deep breath and said," Is it true you had sex with Mr. M3 BMW?"

"What?"

"Is it true you had sex with Mr. M3 BMW?"

"Hell No!"

Now for all of you who don't know who Mr. M3 BMW from my first book is, let me bring you up to speed (you really should read the first book though – shameless plug). Mr. M3 BMW was a good looking guy who died of AIDS a few years back. And after he passed away, Mt. Vernon was filled with rumors of who fucked who and who had what and to be honest with you, I never knew I was part of those rumors. I mean, didn't the streets have enough to talk about when it came to me between the cocaine habit, the excessive drinking and the whoring?

Apparently not.

I continued, "If it will make you comfortable, I will take an AIDS test, but to answer your question, No I never slept with Mr. M3 BMW...and I hope you believe me."

Yeah that's what my mouth said, but in my head I was yelling and cursing. I couldn't believe mother-fuckers could be so cruel. This relationship was going to be some kind of shit to deal with. I looked over at Homeboy, his head was down. What was he thinking? Why was he so Goddamn silent? "Hello, did you hear me, I said No."

He stood up and walked over to me and grabbed my hand. I stood up and he put his head on my shoulder and hugged me... "Of course I believe you...I'm sorry, but..." I covered his mouth with my hand, "Shhhhhh don't apologize for sharing your concerns. I told you, you can ask me anything. Now my rice is burning, I have to go back in the kitchen."

"Ok, I'm going to the corner to get a beer."

I heard the downstairs door shut. I quickly grabbed my cell phone.

And to YOU, Homeboy, I say "Thanks!"

914-424-46## I was calling Azure.

Ring…ring….

Azure answered, "Yeah, what's up?"

"ZiZi can you believe someone told homeboy I fucked Mr. M3 BMW?"

Nonchalantly she replied, "Yeah"

"What do you mean yeah?"

"C'mon Kalico, bitches been hating on you since you came back in town, he's not fucking with Roxanne no more and so you should have known it was gonna be some drama."

I was quiet, Azure was right. She finished, "Bitches always hating on you, you should be used to it."

"How you know it was a female who told him that?"

"Cause niggas don't talk like that."

I heard the door open. "Girl, I gotta go, Homeboy is back from the store."

"Well call me tomorrow, I'm going to get a doobie, my hair is a mess, but after that we can meet up for drinks and seafood somewhere downtown."

"Ok"

"Kalico, shake that shit off and tend to your man, there's always gonna be something because of who you are." She hung up.

And she was correct again. My grandmother always told me, "People

And to YOU, Homeboy, I say "Thanks!"

always remember the bad, never the good."

Azure and me spent a lot of time together, she's gonna be the best man at my wedding when I get married. That's right, I said it, BEST MAN…**No maid of honor for me, 'cause ain't no honor amongst thieves and bitches.** So she's getting the BIG DOG title.

The 2nd Installment of the Kalico Jones Trilogy

And to YOU, Homeboy, I say "Thanks!"

FOUR MONTHS LATER

I'm not feeling well, what's going on with me? Six days in a row, vomiting and severe nausea. I think I'll go to the doctor tomorrow.

Dr. Lavelle's office – Health Center

"Hello Kalico, how are you, long time no see."
"Well I don't know how I'm doing because I'm throwing up, I'm tired and I can't get comfortable when I sleep."
"Really, any night sweats or weight loss?"
"Nope"
"When was your last period?"
"Last month around the tenth."
"You think you may be pregnant?"
"Hmmmm I don't think so."
"Well lets do a pregnancy test."

I was handed a little plastic cup to pee in. I sat in the waiting room until the results came back from the lab. Damn, what if I'm pregnant again? I can't get another abortion. I just can't. You see I made a promise to God that the next time I got pregnant I would keep it. I just couldn't go back on my promise to God.

Why? Because I made a deal with Him.

And to YOU, Homeboy, I say "Thanks!"

THESE ARE MY CONFESSIONS
CONFESSION #1 MY GRANDMOTHERS DEATH

Remember when I told you that what landed me back in Mt. Vernon was the death of my Grandmother? Well me and my Grandmother decided that I would come live with her and find a new job and apartment, but before that living arrangement came to fruition, she died... well...this is my secret ...

When I got the call my grandmother was terminal (going to die) and we – the family – should come to the hospital, I was on my way to get an abortion and so I couldn't make it. I was supposed to get general anesthesia, but I decided to get local because I wanted to go directly to the hospital once the procedure (abortion) was done to see my grandmother for what would be the last time. And I did just that... I went in, paid my 350 dollars and told the doctors I changed my mind, and didn't want to be put to sleep for the procedure. Ok. So the abortion went well – if you can call it that, and I left out shortly thereafter = less than twenty minutes and hurried to the hospital. My cell phone was ringing off the hook because the family wanted to know where I was. No one knew of my whereabouts aside from my mother and the person I was pregnant by (Mr. Diamond Bracelet READ When Gucci Came First – true tales of a tramp). Anyway, I

And to YOU, Homeboy, I say "Thanks!"

hopped out of the taxi and ran into the hospital. When I got to the floor and saw my entire family there, most of them red eyed, and all of them sad. My heart started beating fast. I hurried pass the waiting area to my Grandmothers room and as soon as I put my hand on the door to open it, my Aunt Ethyl came behind me, put her hand on my shoulder and said, "Kalico, Grandma is gone."

It was too late for me to say goodbye.

I've been carrying the guilt from that on my shoulders since. Not like it was my fault she died, because it wasn't. But I had a lot of what ifs and it was hard to really get over the fact that I was not there because I was doing something I really had no business. Something that could have waited, something that had I been protecting myself would not have happened…(taking a deep breath). Why am I trying to sugar coat this? It took me a long time to forgive myself for not being there for her last moment because my black ass was in an abortion clinic for the umpteenth (Ebonics) time. Damn, I think that was the first time I said that aloud, and its been years.

Now back to Dr. Lavelle's office…
"Kalico, your test is negative, you are not pregnant."
"Then what's wrong with me."
"Probably the flu, I'm giving you a prescription for an antibiotic, lets follow up in ten days."
"But it's not even winter."

And to YOU, Homeboy, I say "Thanks!"

"These things happen. You know it doesn't have to be cold outside for you to get the flu."

I left the office and went to Homeboy's house. He would be home shortly and I had to get dinner started. Baked chicken, macaroni & cheese and broccoli ready to go…and I looked and smelled good… all with ten minutes to spare. I heard the downstairs door open.

"Hey Kalico"

"Hey"

"So how'd it go at the doctors?"

"I'm not pregnant." I put my head down and went into the bathroom. I could feel myself getting emotional and I didn't know why. All I know is that I didn't want him to see me upset. I reached to close the bathroom door, but he followed me in and gave me a hug. I sat on the side of the tub, buried my head in my hands and cried.

"Don't worry, its gonna happen, just not right now. But believe me, when it does, you're gonna be a great mom." He wiped my face, "please stop crying."

EXACTLY ONE MONTH AFTER THAT

Guess who's pregnant? Me, yes, Kalico is going to be a mom. I called Azure.

Ring…ring…

ring….

"Hello this is Zi, you know what to do at the beep."

Damn, it was her voicemail. I hung up. I'll just tell her tomorrow. She's gonna flip when I tell her that not only am I pregnant, but I'm KEEPING it.

My promise to God, fulfilled.

This would be the first child for both of us, we're in love and for once, people have stopped talking about me, Thank You Jesus! I guess that trip down south to meet Homeboy's mother did the trick, because …and this is on the Q.T. (quiet tip)…I'm sure that's where I got pregnant.

Okay so now we have to find a new place to live, we have Lamaze, we need life insurance, maternity clothes, and…we have to tell my family.

And to YOU, Homeboy, I say "Thanks!"

We're at my grandmother's house in Lakeview when she (my mother's mother) stood up and made the annual Thanksgiving Toast, "Here's to good food, good friends and a good looking family, and hopefully I can get another great grand out of one of you."

I looked over at my mother in a "no you DIDN'T tell" kind of way – because she was the ONLY one we (me and homeboy) told about the pregnancy, and my grandmother has NEVER said anything like that during the family toast.

My mother looked at me and whispered, "I didn't say anything."
Well I don't know who did, because someone must have told Elaine (my grandmother) about the pregnancy. Because the entire evening all she talked about was baby names, and expanding the family. I knew my mother said something because her ass can't keep a secret to save her life. Fuck it. I wasn't ready, but decided to make the "announcement" and get it over with before my mother bursts.
I stood up, "I'm pregnant!"

No one said a thing. They just kept on talking and laughing as if I didn't say a word. My uncle looked at me as if to say, "again" but he didn't. I knew it was going to take more than the usual, "I'm pregnant" to get their attention…I continued, "and I'm keeping it."

You should have heard the screams and yells coming from my family.

And to YOU, Homeboy, I say "Thanks!"

My Aunt Andrea immediately hugged me and whispered in my ear, "I love you and I'm proud of you." Meanwhile my entire family was still yelling and screaming at the top of their lungs. Shaking Homeboys hand and someone gave another toast, "To the end of the Wild Child!"

And my mother added, "And if you change your mind, I'm here for you."
No she didn't.
Didn't she just hear me say I was keeping it? She even knew about my promise to God. Was she trying to help me get to hell on purpose? I guess I gotta show and prove.

And to YOU, Homeboy, I say "Thanks!"

FIRST SONOGRAM – Month 5 of Pregnancy

"Where is he?"

"Kalico, I'm sure he's on his way."

"Well I can't be late for the doctor. Today we're going to get a sonogram and possibly find out the sex of the baby. Homeboy wants a girl."

I was on the phone with my friend, Mia.

"Girl calm down, he'll be there, just get dressed."

I hung up, got dressed and headed to the health center.

Homeboy was not there.

Alone, but not miserable, I still had a wonderful experience. My nephew Little Joey was there excited to see his cousin "on TV" as he put it. And I, oops I mean, WE were having a girl and life was going great. So great that I didn't even make a big deal about homeboy forgetting the doctors appointment. I know he'd been working longer hours to put our family where we would need to be by the time the baby arrived, and so …I was really ok with it slipping his mind.

Let me stop lying.

And to YOU, Homeboy, I say "Thanks!"

My ass was NOT ok with it, but I was not going to allow it to bother me because I know he had been working a lot lately. There, now that sounds much better. And I guess he thought since I didn't bug from that, he would be able to do whatever the hell he wanted to do, 'cause check out what happened next…

And to YOU, Homeboy, I say "Thanks!"

3AM

3am. Homeboy wasn't home from his night out with the boys.

I called his cell phone. It went straight to voice mail. I didn't leave a message. And why should I? My ass was where I was supposed to be. I know, I know, you're thinking what if something happened right? WRONG! 'Cause his black ass had been hanging out almost every day since I've been on bed rest and I got news for you…if something has happened, fuck it and oh well, 'cause I'm sick of his no show and chronic lateness's.

I heard the lock turn on the door downstairs.

And then…

BOOM!

I jumped out of bed and ran to the stairway. I turned on the light and looked to the bottom of the staircase. This mother-fucker done (Ebonics) fell down the steps. He's drunk AGAIN. Shit. I'm tired of helping his ass up the steps every night, now he's yelling, "Kalico… Kalico!" His drunk ass didn't even realize I was standing at the top of the stairs. So I guess his drunk ass won't remember me turning off this light and getting back in the bed.

Click!

And to YOU, Homeboy, I say "Thanks!"

I turned off the light and walked back into the bedroom and laid down. This nigga can't be serious.

"Kalico…Kalico…you up?"

Homeboy was shaking me, trying to get my attention. I guess his ass sobered up when he fell. "What, stop shaking me."

"You mad at me for being late? I know, I know, I fucked up."

"Damn right you fucked up and I'm…"

He began to talk over me, interjecting, "See what had happened was Sal and his wife had a fight and she kicked him out of the house and then the police gave me a ticket 'cause when I had got there, I couldn't…"

I interrupted his ass, "don't even think about coming in here insulting my intelligence with this weak ass lie," I threw my hand up and in stop like gesture and…

WHAM! He slapped me. No he didn't just slap me? I grabbed my face and yelled, "I'm leaving!"

I went for the phone, he grabbed it and threw it across the room. I grabbed my shoes and ran to the door. He followed and pulled the back of my hair and we both fell down the stairs. Him head first and me, on my ass, thank God for the banister. I was able to grab it during the fall. Homeboys head was bleeding and I had a sharp pain shooting through the bottom of my stomach. I closed my eyes and prayed, "God protect my baby please." I got up, walked back up the steps and went to bed. Homeboy followed. Neither one of us said a

And to YOU, Homeboy, I say "Thanks!"

word. A few hours later he got up, got dressed and went to work. He didn't wake me to say goodbye.

I didn't want him to.

9:40am

Ring…ring…ring…

Ring…ring…ring…

Ring…ring…ring…

Damn, how many times are they gonna let the phone ring and why isn't the answering machine on? I better get the phone, 'cause its obvious the person on the other end is bored. I reached for the phone, "Hello" "Baby, I'm sorry." It was Homeboy sounding pitiful. I guess his conscious was bothering him. He continued, "I love you, please don't leave me."

And hung up.

I sat back on the bed and exhaled. I was faced with a serious decision. I took out a sheet of paper and made a list, it looked something like this:

And to YOU, Homeboy, I say "Thanks!"

<table>
<tr><td>Why Stay</td><td>Why Leave</td></tr>
<tr><td>Both Parents for daughter Stability</td><td>It will happen again</td></tr>
<tr><td>He loves me</td><td></td></tr>
<tr><td>He's sorry</td><td></td></tr>
<tr><td>I love him</td><td></td></tr>
<tr><td>Everyone deserves a second chance</td><td></td></tr>
<tr><td>Shit. I called my mother.</td><td></td></tr>
</table>

I took a deep breath and explained my dilemma…

"What in the hell do you mean he slapped you? Joey, Homeboy slapped your sister!"

Damn, I didn't know my brother was there.

 "I know that mother-fucker didn't put his hand on you…" It was my brother Joey on the phone, he must have snatched the phone from my mother.

"Listen, before you come over here Joey don't ,'cause I'm not leaving. Please let me handle this." I can't believe I said that. I sounded like a fucking idiot.

"You know what Kali, I'm going to let you handle this, but let that nigga know…he is to stay far away from me. And if it happens again, I'M going to handle it…You better tell him."

"Okay, I'll tell him."

"No, not okay and you better let that nigga know."

"Okay"

"Now Ma wants to speak with you."

My mother returned to the phone, "Kalico Renee, I don't know

    The 2nd Installment of the Kalico Jones Trilogy

And to YOU, Homeboy, I say "Thanks!"

what your plan is, but it better work, 'cause I'm not going to stop
your brother next time."
"Okay"

My brother and homeboy only said, "Hi" and "Bye" to each other
after that.

The next few months that followed were riddled with rumors of
Homeboys infidelity, excessive drinking and hanging out. Mt.
Vernon's focus had shifted from me to Homeboy. And he loved it.
Especially when Bunny tried to fix him up with Kelly, you remember
Kelly – my ex best friend from book one? I guess she was still mad at
me for fucking her father.

Oh well…

See the one thing I didn't let bother me was another bitch trying
to give my man some pussy. I mean really, what could Kelly or
anyone else for that matter, do to him that hasn't already been done?
And don't give me that shit about them possibly doing something
BETTER , 'cause in the pussy department, quality is job ONE! And
trust and believe, I'm not bragging. I guess that rumor about me and
Mr. M3 BMW didn't mean shit, 'cause every chance a bitch got to
fuck behind me, they did. Bitches were actually having a blast seeing
me in retirement (pregnant), or at least immobile for nine months.
(I'm sucking my teeth.), little did they know.

And to YOU, Homeboy, I say "Thanks!"

Little did they know I was still calling in favors, big belly and all. Western Unions still coming in cross-country courtesy of Mr. Diamond Bracelet, Mr. Realtor and all the others. A piece of pussy, niggas may remember, but good head, niggas never forget. Cute, smart and on top of my sheet game, I capitalized on my ability to handle my fucking business.

There was just one problem. With me being pregnant, chicks began to show their ass. Every time I ran into someone in the streets, they would make it a point to stop me.

And to YOU, Homeboy, I say "Thanks!"

CHICK NUMBER ONE

Location: 4th Avenue between first and second avenue in front of Regine's clothing store.

Chick no. 1: "Oooohh girl is that a belly? So its true, you're really pregnant."

"Yeah, I guess bitches can eat now."

Chick no. 1: "Ha, ha, you're so funny Kal."

"Come on, y'all know y'all was shook when I touched down after seven years."

Acting like she didn't hear a word I said, she responded , "Invite me to the baby shower okay."

"Yeah, I'll do that."

On her walk away, she stopped, turned around and had the nerve to say, "And Kalico, I hope you get your shape back."

No she didn't! Me get my shape back. Please, that was the LAST thing these bitches wanted. I laughed. I'm not about to let her know that bothered me, I replied, "Girl, I'm sure that won't be a problem, with homeboy working me out at night and the gym he's putting in the house for me to utilize during the day, I'm sure the wonder twins (my ass and tits) will snap back."

Chick no. 1: "But maternity leave is only three months."

And to YOU, Homeboy, I say "Thanks!"

"Maternity leave… (I laughed)…girl I don't work anymore. Homeboy asked me to stop working right after we moved, I think I was just shy of five months." I had this bitch down on the ropes, time to finish her off, "Well, I have to go now, Me and Cynthia are going to the Fendi shop for shoes, take care and oh…look for my baby shower invite.

I got in Homeboys Lexus and pulled off.
Sorry bitch. 3 kids, three baby daddies and one of the kid's acts like wolves are raising him. I don't think she even knows who his father is.
How pathetic.

And to YOU, Homeboy, I say "Thanks!"

BABY SHOWER DAY

Location: Our First house – Mt. Vernon, NY
May 14th, 2000.

My brother Charles and his wife flew in from Mexico. Mi Mi Smith won all the prizes. Black's wife Thea came with DKNY for the baby, My girl from Long Island was there rubbing my stomach – Nettie…I think she's going to be my daughters Godmother. Also there was my oldest and dearest friend Mona with her mom and sister. Homeboy's mom was there, and both of our families. It was nice. It was so nice that I didn't fight with Homeboy about coming in ten o'clock that morning. And chick number one, well, she didn't show…

And rightfully so…seeing as she never did get that invite. Fuck her, and besides that, with all these fake ass bitches in attendance, I'm sure she'll hear about it.

Lots of food, fun and presents…But that wasn't good enough because about an hour into the shower, homeboy = wisdom, a.k.a baby daddy was trying to get his ass out the door. I don't know where he thought he was going, but his mother put a stop to that. I heard her in the kitchen telling him to stay put.

And to YOU, Homeboy, I say "Thanks!"

MOTHER KNOWS BEST

"You are going to stay here with your pregnant wife until this is over."

"She's not my wife."

"Girlfriend, fiancé, baby momma, I don't care, you are not going to embarrass the family by leaving."

"I don't want to be here Mommy, why can't you just leave me alone about this?"

"Why don't you want to be here? What's going on?"

"I accidentally slept with someone she invited, are you happy now…I slept with one of her friends and the girl is here, in our house, at this shower…right now."

(yelling) "You did WHAT?"

Homeboy's eyes were turning red. He was clearly upset. His mother asked him not to tell her which one, but that she better have a need to leave suddenly because her presence was disrespectful to everyone in attendance.

I looked over at homeboy's mother who appeared to be getting sick. I yelled out to her, "Hey mom, are you ok in there?"

She responded, "Yes honey, I'll be in there in one second me and

         The 2nd Installment of the Kalico Jones Trilogy

And to YOU, Homeboy, I say "Thanks!"

your husband are talking."
I continued to mingle with our guests.

Homeboy came into the living room, put his head on my shoulder and said, "Baby, I have to make a run right quick...I have to pick up your surprise...give me about a half hour, I will be right back."
I grabbed his face and smiled, "Ok...I'm going to miss you."

Five minutes later
Ring...ring...ring ...ring...
My mother yelling, "Someone's cell phone is ringing...someone's cell phone is ringing..."
It was Nettie's. She excused herself to the downstairs hallway.
Ten minutes later....

Nettie returned, "Girl I have to go."
"What do you mean you have to go, we're just getting started, I didn't even open the gifts...please stay a while, I haven't seen you and I miss your crazy ass."
"I can't, I have a problem, my sister is in trouble and I have to rush home. I promise, I'll call you as soon as things get settled at home."
Saddened by her sudden departure, I put my head down as we hugged goodbye.
"I love you girl and you better be here when this baby is born...you

know I'm making you her Godmother."
Nettie looked at me with tears in her eyes, "I love you too and I will try my best to be here for you."

She left.

Just then my soon to be mother-in-law came over and said, "I can't believe I'm going to have another granddaughter, I am so excited and you're still all that girl, even with the belly." I smiled. I really loved that lady. She was so sweet and knew just what to say and when to say it. We would spend hours together laughing and talking and one time even crying together. She and I had so much in common.

Well, The party was coming to an end and homeboy still was not back yet. It was well beyond the half hour he promised. But I wasn't upset because I knew he was out doing something for me and so I could put up with the tardiness this time. And besides that, it was a happy day.
Its now almost 7:30pm. And homeboy is just returning from his "half hour" excursion. He handed me a bag. It was from a jeweler. I opened the box to find a nice bracelet and ring. I read the card, "I love you and I'm sorry."

I turned the card over to find the name, location and telephone number of the jeweler...

          The 2nd Installment of the Kalico Jones Trilogy

And to YOU, Homeboy, I say "Thanks!"

It was located in Long Island.

I passed the card and box to his mother…Who tried to act as though she didn't know something she did…"Its beautiful. I love it, girl… lets put it on you!"

"Maybe tomorrow. I'm going to bed now. I know you and your son have a lot to talk about and to be honest, I'm very tired. Its been a long day for me."

I gave her a kiss and hug and extended the same to Homeboy and went to bed. I could hear his mother talking. They were in the guest room, "How could you?"

"Mommy, it just happened, we're both sorry."

"And you took her home? You do know that Kalico is going to figure it out and when she does, she is going to hit the ceiling."

"I know, but maybe she won't."

"She's probably already figured it out."

"You know Kali, if she had a one clue of all this, she would have said something…trust me, she won't know. It was a mistake and it's over."

"You know you can't allow her to make this girl the baby's Godmother, I won't stand for it. You can't let that happen."

"It won't"

"It better not. Now go in there with your wife and relax."

"See you in the morning mommy."

"Sweet dreams honey." I turned over so that I faced the wall.

And to YOU, Homeboy, I say "Thanks!"

Between the hanging out, drinking and possibly fucking one my best friends, I just didn't even want to look at his ass.

I guess whatever he thought the streets had for him was more important to him than being the person he should have been for me at that time.

From that day forward I didn't object when he told me he was going out. I had enough of trying to convince him of the importance of standing by me during my pregnancy. I had enough of trying to show him how much I loved him. If he didn't want to be there for me, then why in the world should I force him?

I mean, once you come to the conclusion that the long stem roses for no reason at all, the jewelry, trips, cars and slow dances in the living rooms of the big house we lived in no longer exist...what do you do?

Nothing.

You prepare yourself for the burn and hope the pain doesn't last too long.

Damn, I hate love.

My dad called me. He wanted to take me out for a father/daughter breakfast. Since I moved into the new house with homeboy, my father made it a point to see me at least once or twice a week for breakfast.

     The 2nd Installment of the Kalico Jones Trilogy

And to YOU, Homeboy, I say "Thanks!"

MONTH # 7 of Pregnancy

Location: Sugar Bowl (5th Avenue & Sanford Blvd, Mt. Vernon)

Smiling and happy to see him, "Hi Daddy!"

"How's my baby girl?"

"Fine Daddy."

"No you're not, I can feel it, what's going on?"

I began to cry, "Daddy me and Homeboy are having problems…he hit me, he's drunk all the time and today he came home at noon. I'm sick of this."

"Kali, come home."

That night I stayed at my father's house. Homeboy came there drunk and crying, pleading for me to return. I went back the next day. But don't ask me why, 'cause every chance he got, he showed his ass. Out constantly drinking and partying with his friends. I knew I had to leave, but didn't want to be a single parent. I just couldn't go through that, not after all those abortions. Not after waiting so long to have a baby. Not after my promise to God, not after all that. What was I going to do? I decided the best way to save our relationship was to move. I found a place across the Tappan zee Bridge in Spring

And to YOU, Homeboy, I say "Thanks!"

Valley, NY.

I called homeboy on his cell phone to tell him the good news.

"Wisdom"

"Yeah, what's up? Is it time? Did your water break?"

"No"

"Good, cause we're watching the game and I've had some drinks. I don't think I'm going to be able to make it home tonight."

"What?"

"I've had some drinks and I don't think I'm going to be able to make it home tonight….and before you get mad, you're the one who told me not to drive when I am drinking, I'll see you in the morning."

He hung up.

He never even gave me a chance to tell him about the apartment.

I called the rental office and did a check by phone for the new place.

I knew he was going to be upset with me for spending four thousand dollars without his permission, but if he wanted to be with me and make this work, then he would move, if not, I would have to see if I could get a refund because at this point I did not want to move without him.

Two days and 17 calls to homeboy later…

Homeboy finally makes it home and before I could get my hands around his neck, he figured he would tell me some kind of fucking story as to why his ass was unable to make it home for not one, but TWO fucking days.

       The 2nd Installment of the Kalico Jones Trilogy

And to YOU, Homeboy, I say "Thanks!"

"Kalico, I was locked up….and…."
"Nigga please, I called your job, you went to work today and yesterday you called out."
"Let me just tell you I tried to call you but you didn't …."
I cut him right off and said, "We're moving to Spring Valley before these streets swallow you, me and our baby. I can't take it anymore, we're going."

At first he didn't say a word. He just looked at me. I guess he was trying to see if I was bluffing, but he could tell by the look on my face I was dead ass serious.
He put his head down, "Its just that I feel like I'm missing something, I don't know what's come over me."
"I don't know what's come over you either, but before this baby comes, you better get your shit together."

I explained to him that I purchased the apartment with his money and that we were moving so I could get peace and quiet. I was tired of living for the streets and surely tired of watching him play me like a fucking piano. He agreed to the move once he saw the apartment and coincidentally we lived in the building adjacent to his friend Derrick.
Damn.

Every day he did whatever he needed to do to get out of being around me. He went to the store – five times a day, he worked overtime on the weekends. He worked on his car. Everyday there was an excuse as to why his black ass couldn't stay in the house. I cooked, cleaned and did what a woman was supposed to do to keep a man, but something had a hold of him. Something that as I write this sentence, I cannot, for the life of me figure out. I felt a little wetness.

"Joey (my older brother), I think I'm peeing on myself, get out of the bathroom," I yelled as I banged on the bathroom door and did the "pee pee" dance.

My brother opened the bathroom door and took a look at me, "Your water broke stupid, lets get in the car…where's homeboy?"

"I don't know, he didn't come home last night…I'm going to call him."

"NO, I'M going to call him, what's his number?" my brother said in an aggravated tone.

I didn't want to give homeboy's number to my brother Joey. You see since Homeboy hit me and since the family knew homeboy was slacking off, not coming home and drinking all the time, they – my family – elected my brother Joey as my "guardian" so to speak, and so he's been at my house almost every day for the past three months.

"Give me his damn number, I'm not going to say anything to him, I'm just going to tell him you're going to the hospital."

My brother picked up the phone to dial homeboys number.

That's when we heard the garage door close.

And to YOU, Homeboy, I say "Thanks!"

It was Wisdom coming in smelling like liquor and wobbling. My brother rolled his eyes. I could tell he was pissed. He grabbed him by the arm and said, "Wisdom, get your ass in the shower and change your clothes, my sister has to go to the hospital and I don't want my niece coming into this world smelling liquor on her fathers breath."

MT. VERNON HOSPITAL

And the entire delivery was mess. Homeboy didn't show up for the ending of the birth process. The next day he didn't show up to sign the birth certificate. He was just a fucking no show all the way around. I was distraught. I called my friend Mia from my hospital bed.

Ring…ring…
Ring…ring…
Ring…
"Hello, Mia" "Hey New Mommy, what's up, how are you and the baby?"
I started crying, "Mia what is wrong with him? He didn't even show up to the hospital."
"What do you mean, he didn't show up to the hospital?"
"I mean, he dropped me off, took my brothers car and no one has heard from him since. He hasn't even been to work."
 "Oh my goodness, I hope nothing happened to him, have you tried his cell phone?"
"Its off. Straight to voicemail, he's not answering it."
"Well calm down, let me make some calls, see if anyone has seen

him."

"Ok"

I hung up.

And no, it wasn't okay. This was the prelude to my revelation. Knowing my ass had to not only exit, but exit with a kid. But first, I had to dust off my degree in Business Management and find my black ass a job. And I did just that in a matter of three weeks. I had to find a quick way to make money, save money and make a run for it. I landed a job at a big name telecommunications company.

From Spring Valley to Mt. Vernon to Rye Brook, that was my daily commute. Do you know how long of a commute that is? Its over two hours. But a determined woman will do what is necessary to take care of her child(ren). The only person I could trust with my daughter, lived in Mt. Vernon. She was a former neighbor and she and her family immediately took my daughter in as their own.

"ROCK-A-BYE BABY... ON THE TREE TOP...WHEN THE WIND BLOWS THE CRADDLE WILL ROCK"

"What the fuck are you doing?"

"I'm singing to the baby."

"Well shut the fuck up, I'm trying to sleep"

"What? I'm trying to get her to go back to sleep, why don't you do something useful and help me out."

Homeboy got up and went into the living room. And from that day until the day I left, he would sleep there every night. That is on the nights he decided to come home.

I can't believe I'm stuck here, in the house, with a baby, while HIS ass is out running the streets. I have no money, no food and I'm all the way in Spring Valley.

I called my friend Monet. She left her job and came right over, handed me $100.00 (of which I haven't paid her back to this date) and proceeded to give me the advice that every woman in my situation gets from that one girlfriend, who even though you are down in the

And to YOU, Homeboy, I say "Thanks!"

dumps, feels she has to give you in order to **KEEP IT REAL...**
"Girl you need to leave his ass! This shit is crazy, in the house with a newborn and no money, he can't be serious!" she continued...
"Where's the food? Where's the pampers?"
That's when it HIT me, my ass needed to put together that FUCK YOU money quick. I had to not only exit, but exit with a kid. Where did this go wrong?
I checked the time; it was 1 O'clock in the afternoon, is he okay? And if he is okay, where is he?

The phone rang.
Ring...ring...
"Hello" (it was a famous R&B singer)
"Yo what up Kalico, yo "Wiz" (short for Wisdom), just left my house, he's on his way home, aight?"

I said okay and hung up the phone. I was on fire. How DARE Mr. Famous R&B Singer call my house to tell me that MY MAN was on his way home at 1 O'clock in the afternoon. Where in the hell was he all night? I put the baby in her crib and waited for him to open the door. It's now 2:30pm and homeboy is just walking in the house! He's drunk and shit...looking pitiful, talking about, "I know...I know...I fucked up, I'm sorry...you mad?
"

I took a deep breath, no this nigga did not just ask me if I was mad, he must have bumped his fucking head on the way upstairs. I closed my eyes and thought to myself...I should slap his ass but he's so drunk he probably wouldn't feel it. I will be calm...I will not hit him...I will just leave...I will be calm...I will not hit him...I will just leave...I will be calm...I will not hit him...I will just leave.

I looked at him and in a damn near whisper said, "Yes, I am mad, I'm furious, you're a father now, we are a family, this is crazy...I'm leaving!"

And to YOU, Homeboy, I say "Thanks!"

TWO WEEKS LATER I WAS GONE!

I'm glad I left Homeboy because when you are with someone that you have fantasies of poisoning, its time to go. Ha ha ha. I'm laughing now, but I tell ya, I was this close (putting my pointy finger and thumb as close together as possible without them touching), to poisoning his ass.

The day I left will always be an embedded memory. You see my friend, or shall I say former friend, Miss Mattress tester from Hempstead (Nettie) was there visiting and she and I did everything together. She rubbed my stomach during my pregnancy, she cleaned for me when my belly got too big for me to bend and lift things, she even asked me to be my daughters Godmother, and…. She fucked my child's father the day I left. But from my understanding, their fucking partnership began well before the day I left (retreat to the Baby Shower where she had to suddenly leave and then homeboy comes back with a gift for me from a jeweler in Long Island, him telling his mother that he "accidentally" slept with one of my friends, etc.).

That's right I said it and I will put it out there because since everyone is so damn grown, they need to be accountable for their actions. The day I left I turned to Miss Mattress Tester (Nettie) and said, "I'm leaving, let me drop you off."

She turned me to and replied, "Homeboy is taking me home, that's ok."

"He is?"

"Yeah, you just do what you have to do."

I called my cousin Mike and left, but not before I busted out the windows of his car.

The next day was cold. Colder than usual, even for February and my daughter was running a fever. I took her to the doctor.

"Miss Jones, your daughter has an ear infection, keep her warm, give her this antibiotic and bring her back in five days."

I called Homeboy who convinced me to come home. I did just that. I couldn't go house to house with a seven month old now, especially since she was sick, I just couldn't. So I get back to the house and find out from a neighbor that Miss Mattress tester just left. She had been there every bit of the day and a half I had been gone and the property owners had come to see me because they had gotten several complaints of lewd behavior, weed smoke and loud music.

Damn, he just partied the entire time we were gone. There was little hope for this relationship. And that little bit of hope left when….

And to YOU, Homeboy, I say "Thanks!"

TWO DAYS AFTER THAT...
I RETURNED HOME

February 11, 2001

"Kalico, we have to talk."

"What's up"

"I'm not happy with you two being here. I feel like I'm missing something, like I'm trapped."

"You two. What does the baby have to do with this Wisdom?"

"I just think I'm missing something."

"So you want us to leave?"

"Yes" And just like that, he = homeboy = baby daddy = wisdom and his brother packed up me and our daughters belongings and put them in my car. I went from house to house with my daughter for three weeks. It was the saddest thing you could imagine. Being homeless with a child, when the father is living lovely.

That shit was disgusting. Shame on him.

Me and my daughter we really homeless. I couldn't believe it. A friend of mine offered to take us in for a few days. Brenda and Reggie. We stayed in their guest room in the basement of their house for three days. And for three days Brenda and her boyfriend Reggie would

And to YOU, Homeboy, I say "Thanks!"

watch my daughter as I sat on the floor of their bathroom and cried. I was so hurt. I wouldn't wish that feeling on an enemy and believe me, I've had plenty of enemies over the years.

Three days with Brenda and Reggie. Then two days with the babysitter and her family. And it probably could have been one week until the police showed up at their door interrupting their sleep at almost 5am. They were coming to arrest me. They took me out of their house in handcuffs during a snow storm. Homeboy had called them and told them I went to his job. And I sure did. I went straight to his job and threw my daughters stroller on the hood of his Lexus and posted a note in the snow that said, "Your daughter needs a snowsuit!" I got back in my car and left the scene. I did it so quick no one in the house knew I had went out.

After I was released from Misdemeanor hold, I returned to the sitter's house, she wanted to talk with me about the incident. As soon as I walked into her house, her and her husband called me into their kitchen to talk, "Kalico, we're sorry…but you can't stay here anymore if you are going to continue to cause trouble for yourself. But the baby, she can stay."

"No she can't stay. But thanks for the offer." I gathered our belongings and packed them back into my Nissan Sentra and left. I went by my aunt's house. She gave me the newspaper and we went through it in search of a place for me and my daughter to live.

And to YOU, Homeboy, I say "Thanks!"

YONKERS 10701

I found a place that would not only take a deposit, but would also allow me to move in a few days early. I called homeboy and asked him if he could move me and the baby's stuff out of storage. He did just that, but I don't think it was because he wanted to help. I just think it was because he wanted to know where we were going to be living. When I informed my mother of my need for money, she came right away, wrote a check directly to the landlord and me and my little one were set. Or so I thought. Until Homeboy found out I was "dating" Young Buchanan.

Buchanan, he picked me up every morning, drove me to the sitter and then took me to work. He picked me up when work was over, drove me to the sitter and then took me home. He knew I was struggling and assisted me with things I needed for the baby and myself. Pampers, no problem. Food, no problem. Milk...I didn't even have to ask, he was good to us like that and for that I am forever grateful.

Pulling in the driveway of my new place, and I notice homeboys car. I quickly got the baby out of the car seat, said goodbye to Buchanan

And to YOU, Homeboy, I say "Thanks!"

and made my way in the house where I would find homeboy sitting on my bed watching television.

A startled me yelled, "What are you doing in my house?"

"I can come anywhere my daughter lives…what happened to your little boyfriend. He didn't want to come in?"

"That's not my boyfriend and what are you worried about it for? You're with everyone you can find…so don't start minding my fuckin' business."

 "My daughter is my business and I don't want her around another nigga. You got that?"

"Whatever…I just worked ten hours and I don't have the energy to argue with you…since you're here, can you stay for a minute, so I can take a bath?"

"Yeah"

And I got undressed and ran a nice, hot bath. Something I haven't been able to do with regularity since becoming a full time single parent. Its just showers and jump into my clothing, sometimes without even putting on lotion. Ahhh, it was so relaxing. And then here comes homeboy in the bathroom talking about how much he missed me and his daughter. He began to rub my back, started talking about how good I've been looking lately and that if I were to date anyone to please let it be someone who did not live in Mt. Vernon. Can you believe it. HE wanted to me to RESPECT HIS ass. Ha ha ha.

I got out of the tub, "Your ass is supposed to be watching the baby…

And to YOU, Homeboy, I say "Thanks!"

not in here trying to fuck me Wiz."

"The baby is in her crib sleeping."

"Oh good. Now if you'll excuse me, I would like to put on some clothes."

"I've seen that ass before."

And before I could respond, he had his mouth on my breasts, his hands up my towel and I was feeling no shame. I let the towel drop and we made love right there on the floor of my bathroom. It was great and it was something I needed. . . PROOF that he still cared for me. Yeah right, 'cause as soon as it was over, he was being paged by his "job."

Nigga please.

For the remainder of the week, my calls to homeboy went unreturned, no matter what the content of the message I left was...

"The baby needs milk" – Unreturned

"The baby needs pampers" – Unreturned.

 "The baby is sick" – Unreturned.

"The sitter had an emergency, can you go get the baby." -you guessed it...Unreturned.

Strapped for cash and bitter, I went to the nearest child support enforcement office and filed for support for my daughter. If he wasn't going to man up on his own, then we'll see how he feels when the white man tells him how he is going to spend his paycheck. I didn't hear from homeboy for two weeks.

"Ring....ring...."

And to YOU, Homeboy, I say "Thanks!"

"Hello this is Kalico, thank you for calling Telecom, how can I help you?"

I was at work. On my second written warning for lateness. My daughter had gotten sick from us going from house and my job didn't give a damn either. As a matter of fact, they used my situation against me. Each time I needed to take a day off to take my daughter to the doctor, they wrote me up. I began to have panic attacks and had to go on disability, shortly after this phone call.

"Good morning, thank you for calling Telecom, this is Kalico Jones, how may I help you?"

"Yeah bitch, you taking me to court now. You ain't gonna get shit…"

It was homeboy. I guess he was mad about that subpoena for child support court. Oh well. Fuck him, "Please do not call my job with this bullshit. And yeah, I'm gonna get your fucking money. Fuck you."

"Fuck me? That's why I fucked Nettie, bitch."

"Oh really, well you better go see a doctor then."

I hung up the phone to notice my supervisor standing over my shoulder. "Kalico, may I speak with you for a moment, in my office?"

I followed Stacey to her office. "Sit down Kalico…(she exhaled) tell me what's going on with you…this is off the record. I just need to know. I'm noticing you've been out a lot recently."

   The 2nd Installment of the Kalico Jones Trilogy

And to YOU, Homeboy, I say "Thanks!"

I began to cry. I told Stacey the entire story down to and including homeboy calling my job yelling and cursing at me. Stacey was attentive. She was caring…and she was….

A FUCKING BIG MOUTH!

Everybody who worked on the third floor of Telecom knew my fucking business. The bitch told everyone. And I mean everyone. And they – the mangers - had a fucking field day talking about me and my problems. I was viewed the girl with the fur coat and problems. It was like I was naked every time I went to work.

And to YOU, Homeboy, I say "Thanks!"

I'M BREATHING HARD...MY HEART IS RACING...WHATS HAPPENING TO ME?

I grabbed the wall in the ladies room, gasping for air… (screaming) "Someone please help me, I don't know what's going on with me, help!"

A girl came out the stall. She was from Yonkers. Shari. "Kalico, are you okay, do you want me to get a nurse…call an ambulance, she's having some kind of attack!"

She held my hand and said, "You're gonna be okay. I heard what's going on with you. You'll be just fine. I'm a single mom and you can get through this. If he's acting up, then fuck him. You have to learn how not to focus on him."

"You know my business too?"

"Kalico, we all know. And just as you think people are laughing at you, most of us are not. You have to be strong for your daughter. Look to your daughter for strength if you can't find it within yourself."

Just then the ambulance came and took me to Westchester County Medical Center, I had an anxiety attack and was placed on mental disability for three months. The day after I returned to telecom I was fired. THANK GOD!

And to YOU, Homeboy, I say "Thanks!"

One month after that, the President of the company was indicted on Fraud charges and they filed for bankruptcy. The majority of the people who taunted me lost their jobs, pensions, 401K, all of it. I don't want to say good for them, but if I didn't…I wouldn't be keeping it REAL. Good for them and fuck 'em too! 'cause I hated them. Talking about me like that. And since I had unemployment and one thousand, count it ONE thousand bucks a month in child support, I was fine. And Homeboy, he was just fine too.

And to YOU, Homeboy, I say "Thanks!"

HE WAS DATING A WOMAN WHO LIVED AROUND THE CORNER FROM MY NEW APARTMENT

What a joke!

Another new apartment you ask? Yup because although my calls to Homeboy went unreturned, that didn't stop him from coming to my house at night to see if there were any unfamiliar cars in my driveway, which coincidentally anytime there was, the vehicles were vandalized. This would happen over and over again. And time and time again me and my "visitor" would have to contact the Yonkers police department to report busted car windows and "mysterious" dents and scratches. And with my landlords living upstairs, an elderly couple, whose children felt it was not in the best interest of their parents for me to continue my residency there, I was asked to move OUT two months after moving IN.

At least they returned my security deposit. I would need it to help pay for my new apartment on 222nd in the Bronx. The Lady around the corner from me, let's call her Jessica was a disaster. She was older, been around the block more times that one can admit to (and that's a lot coming from a person like me) and had five, count 'em FIVE mother fucking kids. Five kids all of whom he helped her support

And to YOU, Homeboy, I say "Thanks!"

and all the while never once did he check in on his daughter before, during or after our child's hospitalization for clinical pneumonia, or just even to say hello. I decided that since I couldn't get him to do the right thing, maybe I could appeal to Jessica, so…I went to her house.

The fucking dungeon projects of the South Bronx, two bedrooms and five kids, you do the math. She had my fucking living room furniture … The bitch had all my shit, including the fucking plants. A dark skinned heavyset woman came to the door, "Can I help you?"

"Yeah, are you Jessica?"

"Yes, why?"

"I'm Kalico, please tell Wisdom his daughter needs pampers, food and where is the child support…(I pushed the door and walked in)… matter of fact, is he here?"

She replied, "No he didn't get in from work yet, but I'll tell him what you said."

"And please let him know, I will be back."

"Again Kalico…right?... I'll tell him you came by, but he's going to be mad when he finds out you came here."

"You damn right he's gonna be mad and you're going to be lonely because now that he knows I know where he is laying his head, he won't be here too often, take care."

And me and my daughter made our way down that pissy ass stairwell to the first floor landing, almost fell coming out the entrance way due to the broken step and door hinge. What a life! And for one

And to YOU, Homeboy, I say "Thanks!"

month that became MY LIFE.

Weekly trips to Jessica's house, each time becoming more frustrated than the next. Each time with my daughter on my hip, and each time walking away with a feeling that I knew her from some where. I was sure I'd seen her somewhere before. I called my friend Juanita, who came to my house that night just to sit with me while I cried. Juanita was a good friend to me during my trials with homeboy and for that I am forever thankful to her. Juanita held my hand as I shook my head back and forth and cried, "Kalico, there is nothing homeboy can do for her or any other woman that he has not done for you... you have to pull yourself together, don't let the streets see you like this, enough is enough."

"Juanita, I just want to beat his ass. I just want him to feel the hurt I am feeling. I just need to know what is more important than his daughter, do you have any idea how this is consuming me?"

"I know sweetie, but you have to stop going to this woman's house, please. You're torturing yourself and you can't go on like this."

Juanita rubbed my back and took the baby into the bedroom for a nap.

I picked up the phone and called homeboy. His voicemail came on. I left a message, "This is Kalico, I don't know what could be more important than your daughter, but its obvious she is not enough for you, so, I am not going to bother you again...take care."

I hung up.

And to YOU, Homeboy, I say "Thanks!"

And I didn't bother him again…for THREE and a half weeks, I didn't call, I didn't go to Jessica's house, I didn't bother a soul. I didn't eat, I didn't sleep, I didn't cry. All I did was feed, wash and play with my daughter and think of ways I could torture homeboy. Against my better judgment and promise to Juanita, I returned to Jessica's house. She came to the door and before she could say anything to me, I said, "I'm not here to bother you, I just want to know if you have seen my daughter's father, I need to speak with him, its important."

"Kalico, he and I are no longer together, he lives with Kelly."

"Kelly who?"

"Kelly the person I believe he said you screwed her father or something like that."

"What?"

"Yeah, they are together now and the other day when you let his aunt spend time with your daughter, she took her over to Kelly's house so they spent time together as a family…I told him that wasn't right, but he insists on getting revenge because child support is taking most of his money."

I began to breath hard, I grabbed Jessica to prevent from falling…

"Kalico are you okay, Ray Ray (her oldest son) bring me a glass of water and a chair quick."

She handed me the glass of water and I splashed it on my face, I was sick, but I was not about to drink shit from her house, with all the things I have done to her, that water could have come from the toilet!

Sick but not stupid, I yelled, "I'm going to kill him!"

I turned to leave, but something about Jessica bothered me. I told you I had a weird feeling when I first saw her, as though we may have known each other and so I took this opportunity to ask, "Jessica, do we know each other? I have this feeling I've seen you before."

She replied, "I'm the one you rolled up on that day on the boulevard. I was talking to your baby's father…I was the one who kissed your daughter on the cheek and you jumped out the car."

"THAT was you? So you've been fucking with him for what, a year or so now…Oh how I am going to enjoy what I am about to do to him."

I immediately drove into Mt. Vernon, thinking about what Jessica just told me. I was furious that homeboy would play me out like this. Me and his daughter. How could he? And now he's fucking with Kelly! I drove down ninth avenue, I had to see if it was true. I got out of my car and rang Kelly's bell. No answer. Shit.

And to YOU, Homeboy, I say "Thanks!"

NOW WHAT?

I know…I got back in the car and before I knew it, I was on my way to Kelly's job. And low and behold she was there. I walked right in the office and directed a question to her, "Is my daughter's father living with you?"

And with a smirk on her face, she replied, "Yeah."

"Did he bring my daughter to your house?"

Still smirking, she responded, "Yeah, and I even changed the little bitch's pamper."

My heart almost jumped straight out of my chest. I thought to myself, I should just beat the shit out of this bitch right here, right now, right in this fucking Government building, but nah…She was protected by the glass partition and so that would be a waste of time. Or would it?

I began to talk myself out of possibly being charged with not only beating her ass, but fucking up Government property. I decided that since I've already beaten her ass once, it wasn't worth the criminal record. And besides that, so many women have been up to that office threatening to beat her ass over their men…that it wouldn't really make a difference and more so than that…homeboy wasn't MY man anymore, my beef was only about the kid going to her house,

And to YOU, Homeboy, I say "Thanks!"

nothing else.

As I turned to leave, I walked back toward the glass partition that protected her ass from getting punched in the mouth, "You should have never fucked with my daughter!" She stuck up her middle finger and picked up the phone to make a call. I could hear her talking to homeboy. I even heard her laughs as I made my way down the hall. Yeah, she was a real comedian behind all the glass partition. A real Wanda Sikes. I know I know, I should have slapped the shit out of her for making a comment like that about my daughter, but truth be told, I had a bigger score to settle.

I made a left at the end of the hall and found my way down the emergency exit staircase because there were cameras in the elevators. As I got to the final landing, I put my sweat hood over my head and tightened the strings, jumped in my car and went back to her house where I would find homeboy rolling a blunt = marijuana in a cigar with his friend Benny. I jumped out of the car, "How could you fucking do this to me?"

Homeboy ran backward toward the steps and fell. I ran up on him yelling, "How could you bring my child to this bitch's house?"

"I live here." He yelled back and that's when I lost it.

I kneeled down, grabbed a rock, held it in my hand real tight and punched him dead in the face. I think it startled him because he dropped his blunt, grabbed me by my jacket and threw me against a Cadillac truck parked outside, and it was ON! We were in the street

And to YOU, Homeboy, I say "Thanks!"

fighting like two wild animals in the jungle eyeing the same piece of meat. It was messy, it was embarrassing and it was bloody. When Homeboy realized my eye was cut, he ran into the house screaming, "You're going to jail bitch."

I got in my car, went around the corner to my girlfriend's hair salon and called the police. He was arrested for assault, and endangering the well-being of a minor. My daughter was in the car with me during the altercation. That was on Friday. Saturday after waking up with a terrible headache and bloodshot eye, I made my way to the local emergency room where I was told I had severe damage to my left retina and I would need surgery in a few years because it would eventually affect my vision. SHIT!

I rested the following day and on Monday I went to the local police department where he was being held on bail to speak with the District Attorney.

So I'm standing at the window, waiting for someone to take my victim impact statement and low and mother fucking behold, the same cop who arrested him just two days prior was sent out into the hall to arrest ME. I had my daughter with me, and so I was a mess. I asked the officer what would happen if I didn't cooperate and I was told that they would issue a warrant and have the Bronx police kick in my door.

For the record and in the spirit of keeping it REAL, the police officer didn't even want to arrest me. But being as Kelly told them this

And to YOU, Homeboy, I say "Thanks!"

elaborate story about how I not only threatened her, but I went to her place of employment, they had to unfortunately arrest me and then let the court sort the story out. The officer assured me the process would be swift, and that I would be reunited with my daughter in less than one hour.

I quickly found one of my family members to take my daughter to the McDonalds across the street from the courts, just so that child protective services would not be called, since at that point BOTH of her parents would be in the custody of the New York State Department of Corrections. How pathetic.

Homeboy sitting in one cell and me in the other with all the crack heads I knew from way back when I was selling coke in front of the projects.

There was only ONE thing that would work in my favor: since I had never been in trouble the only thing I could be charged with was a violation, which meant there would be no probation, no jail time, no criminal record or finger prints taken…just a stay away order.

Which didn't mean shit to me.

I began to think. How did it get to this? The very person I had a restraining order against for THREE years (Kelly) had now obtained one against me. It was a mess, or so I thought until the cops showed up at my door in the Bronx to serve me with court papers not even one week later. Homeboy and Kelly were suing me for custody of MY daughter. And if that wasn't enough, he also petitioned family court to grant him a restraining order against me based on the harassment

     The 2nd Installment of the Kalico Jones Trilogy

And to YOU, Homeboy, I say "Thanks!"

allegations that were currently against me in Criminal court with regards to his now "girlfriend" and GOT it!

So…follow me now: I had a restraining order against Kelly for three years, and she now had one against me, I had a restraining order in criminal court against homeboy and he now had one against me in family court…and to top that off, he was trying to sue me for custody of my daughter on the grounds of being "unstable" and "psychotic."

Its official, this break up has now CONSUMED me.

Every chance they (homeboy and Kelly) got, they flaunted their relationship in my face. Driving by my house, which by the way was a good thirty minutes from their house and a whole different borough. Whenever I was out, they always made their way to wherever I was. And although I knew they only did that to fuck with me…I ALLOWED it to fuck with me. Both of them did everything in their power to make me go the fuck off and they came really close to their goal.

And to YOU, Homeboy, I say "Thanks!"

FRUSTRATED AND DEPRESSED I PICKED UP THE PHONE AND CALLED MY OLD COCAINE CONNECT

Ring…ring…

ring…

"Hello, its Kali"

"Yeah, what's up Kali? Is there something I can do for you?"

"Yeah, can you bring my old usual?"

"No, but if that's what you want…then I will do it."

"Its what I want. I'm at on 222nd, you remember where, right?"

"Of course, I'll be there in ten minutes."

Five minutes later my bell rang. I put the baby in her crib and I unlocked the door to relapse. I handed my "connect" the money, grabbed my package and quickly closed the door. I didn't want to make eye contact with him. I went into the room. The baby was sleeping. I sat at my kitchen table, opened the package and before I knew it, I had sniffed the entire thing. Forty dollars worth of cocaine, up my nose after being clean for two and a half years. I felt so fucking bad. How could I let this shit get to me like this? I was a mother now.

And to YOU, Homeboy, I say "Thanks!"

Was my daughter not a good enough reason for me to keep it together?

Thirty days of being high. I began to lose weight. I was irritable and every time I turned around I was getting papers in the mail from court: child support, criminal court, family court…court…court… court. At one point I contemplated suicide. The cocaine had begun to make its way back into my life on a daily basis. One time I even left my daughter in the house sleeping while I drove twenty minutes away for cocaine and cigarettes. When I returned to the apartment I would find my upstairs neighbor knocking on my door. My daughter had awakened during my "run" for drugs.

"Oh, what's up Teresa? Can I help you with something?"

"Kali, your daughter has been up screaming and crying for a half hour. You left her in the house by herself?"

"I just ran to the store."

"Well next time you want to just run to the store, bring her upstairs so I can keep an eye on her, you know you can go to jail for that shit."

"Sorry, won't happen again."

I entered the room to find my daughter turning red from crying and being hungry. I picked her up. She went for my breast… "Sorry stinky, mommy cannot breast feed you anymore." I prepared a bottle and rocked her to sleep. I was so weak during the trials that my ass gave up BREAST feeding my baby to get high.

And to YOU, Homeboy, I say "Thanks!"

Ugh, the sound of that is sickening to say the very least.

My mother called me the next day. She was concerned about me because she hadn't seen me or the baby in about one month.

Ring…ring…

"Hello."

"Hey Kali, its mom, how are you?"

"Ok, just trying to have some time to myself, what's up?"

"Well me and your brothers were thinking about coming to see you and the baby. We wanted to talk to you about an idea we came up with."

"Ok, well just let me know when."

"We're coming across the GW Bridge right now, we should be there in twenty minutes."

Shit!

Twenty minutes. My apartment was a MESS. I looked crazy. Was up all night getting high and I looked like it. My daughter was not bathed. Her hair was not combed and I haven't done laundry in weeks. There was NO food in the house aside from baby food and milk and I lost about twenty pounds. I know, I know…I can blame the weight loss on stress. And I'm sure I can get this house cleaned and aired out from the cigarette smoke in twenty minutes.

I ran to the living room, opened the window. I ran into the bedroom, opened the window. Washed the baby in the bathroom. Combed her hair into a ponytail. Washed the dishes. Damp mopped the kitchen floor. Took all the dirty clothes off the couch and threw them in the

          The 2nd Installment of the Kalico Jones Trilogy

And to YOU, Homeboy, I say "Thanks!"

hallway closet and shut it tight. I washed my face, underarms and found a pair of homeboy's old sweatpants and put them on with a t-shirt. Dug out my cosmetic bag and put on makeup…I was done and I think I looked okay.

Buzz…Buzzz.

It was the doorbell and in walked Joey, Charlie and my Mother. They each gave me a hug and my mother took the baby. We sat down in the living room. I turned on the TV. But instead of watching it, I watched my brother Joey make eye contact with my mother…SHIT! I forgot to get rid of the ashtray. Damn, I'm busted.

My mother spoke, "Kali, you look…I don't know…like you are not taking care of yourself."

"I'm fine ma."

"Kal are you doing drugs again?"

"Joey, don't say that to your sister!" my mother yelled.

My brother continued, "Listen, someone has to ask since we didn't really know for sure last time with her. Its hat you want to say anyway ma, so let's just put it out there."

"Kali we got a call from your landlord. You left the baby in the house by herself the other day for almost one hour. You cannot do this. I am told this may not have been the first time you have done this in the middle of the night."

"I'm going to kick her ass when I catch her, you do know that right? You should not have told me she called you. Why would she call you in the first place?"

And to YOU, Homeboy, I say "Thanks!"

"Kali, its better she called me than the police. The baby is screaming. It's the middle of the night. She didn't know if something happened to you. The only reason she didn't call the police was because she noticed your car was not in the driveway. So really, she did YOU a favor. YOU should not be upset with her."

"Whatever" I sucked my teeth.

"And so I'm going to ask you again…are you doing drugs Kal?" My brother Joey determined to get me to lie to him.

I mean they saw the way I looked. They could tell I was doing something, right? I replied, "No I am not doing drugs."

"Well I hope not, because you know Mrs. Federico (family attorney) is asking that homeboy be tested for drug use and so that means YOU will be tested as well."

"You don't know what you're talking about Joey, please."

"Please my ass. Listen…If you are doing drugs again you better stop because if anything happens to my niece I'm going to fuck you up."

"Okay that's enough…we didn't come here for that Joey and you are not going to beat up your sister." My mother said, trying to keep everyone from becoming excited.

"Yes, that is what we came for. Kali why do you think we didn't call first? Look at her ma…she looks a mess. Ashtrays laying around. She's in here smoking with my niece in here. You ain't saying nothing about it. Acting like my sister don't need help. That's what messed her up before. Everyone acting like they didn't see her fucking up. Well I see it and I want us to address it because there is more to lose now that she's a mother!"

And to YOU, Homeboy, I say "Thanks!"

My mother stood up and asked to speak with me in private.

We went into the bedroom. She put her arm around me, "Listen…If you need help, its okay. We will get you whatever help you need, but you have to be honest with me. Are you getting high?"

And I looked my mother right in the face, without blinking and LIED, "No ma, I am not getting high. I am stressed and yes, I sometimes smoke cigarettes at night when the baby is sleeping in her room, and maybe have a drink or two, but I am NOT getting high."

"I hope not Kali because your brother is right. When you get into court on next week, the judge is going to order both you and Homeboy to be drug tested. Now from my understanding, that could be hair follicles or it could be urine or a blood sample. I don't know. But we need you to be prepared, please. Now I am going to take your word for it and assume we are not going to have any surprises in court on Tuesday, okay?"

"Ok."

We rejoined my brothers in the living room.

"I think you should consider moving," said my brother Charlie. He kept talking, "I don't like you being so close to Mt. Vernon. I don't like you being in this area. You should reconsider Ma's offer to get you out of here once and for all. There is nothing here for you, and besides. I'm starting to become scared for your safety."

"What does that mean?"

"It means this thing between you and homeboy has gotten so ugly. Ya'll running around here doing things to each other every chance you get. I have a terrible feeling one of you is going to be severely hurt by the other. Its not a good feeling for me at all when I think about the situation you both have caused and contributed to."

"Charlie, you don't have to worry about me, I will be just fine."

He began to cry, "But you're my sister and I love you. I'm just scared for my niece. Please consider mommy's offer. Kali, you need to leave."

And at the advice of my mother AND brothers, I prepared myself to move. Why should I stick around anyway? I had no real ties to anyone in Mt. Vernon. My Grandmother has passed away. My father was now living in North Carolina and everyone in my family that truly mattered (no offense to anyone in my family because they know I love them all), was not a resident of Mt. Vernon. It was time for me to move, once again.

And to YOU, Homeboy, I say "Thanks!"

I'M GOING BACK AND FORTH TO COURT CRIMINAL COURT ONE WEEK FAMILY COURT THE NEXT

So we get to family court, it's the day of the trial and he attempts to use his girlfriends Criminal court allegations against me in family court to prove my "instability." But since I haven't plead guilty, those charges will not and CANNOT be used against me and the judge grants me sole custody, legal, physical, etc. and child support, of which I already had, he just never paid. What did he get?

Alternate Sundays to visit his child and the right to pay his fucking child support. The judge also lifted the restraining order against me and three weeks later, I got the fuck outta dodge – RELOCATED! But in the meantime and in between it being time for me to move, I was arrested two more times: Criminal contempt first degree = a felony, Kelly claimed I called her house and threatened her and Criminal contempt second degree = a misdemeanor, this time I was fingerprinted, photos were be taken, and bail would be set in the amount of 5,000 dollars, damn I'm in a mess.

I was bailed out so quick, the court officer barely had enough time to take my photo and fingerprints. . . Thanks again Mom!

And to YOU, Homeboy, I say "Thanks!"

The criminal contempt second degree would be in retaliation to a notice posted outside the homes and on all the cars of everyone in a three block radius of where they lived, I believe began something like this:

Attention, attention…. Kelly is a whore, Homeboy is a dead beat dad, etc….

And this notice made its way around the entire Mt. Vernon. Up Third Street, down Fourth Avenue and through the Post Office = were gossip travels like brush fires in the state of California and everyone assumed it was the handy work of the bitter ex baby momma = me. But it was not (that's my story and I'm sticking to it).

During this time of repeated detainments, I would have to adhere to the court ordered visitation schedule and take my daughter to Goshen, NY for what would be six consecutive Thursday afternoon visits with her father. On the third week, I was told the case had been dismissed and that I did not have to bring her there any longer. When I inquired as to why, the appointed "third party" informed me that Homeboy never showed for any of the visits. And that it would be the recommendation of the "third party" that he seek counseling prior to engaging in any activity with his daughter. In other words, "he just wasn't interested in seeing her." And why would he be? He was too busy being a father to Kelly's children, too busy taking the kids on vacations, and amusement parks, etc. to worry about how

And to YOU, Homeboy, I say "Thanks!"

his daughter was doing. And as I write this sentence she has seen her father less than 10 times in what will equate to being Five years (2/06). But don't feel sorry for HER, 'cause I'm HER mother and so you can put your money on me all the time. She is doing just great, excelling in school, she is beautiful inside and out and despite everything I have done to incorporate him and his family into her life, THEY ARE STILL NO SHOWS.

And to YOU, Homeboy, I say "Thanks!"

I'M FREE!!!!!!!

After being told I didn't have to bring my daughter for the visits anymore. I relocated, yes, Kalico moved back to New Jersey to just really get my head on straight. And figure out what I am going to do as far as my life is concerned, how was I going to pick up the pieces of my life and keep a positive outlook during my criminal trials. For 8 months I went back and forth to court twice per month while awaiting a trial date for something I did not do. And Kelly never showed. There was always some excuse as to why she could not show up, until eventually the district attorney dropped the charges. Bail money returned, photos and fingerprints destroyed, per court order, and Kalico Jones was finally FREE.

Free for ONE entire year of no contact with anyone from Mt. Vernon, including Homeboy.

Free, Free, free, until super bowl weekend, 2003 when I got a call from Homeboy stating that he wanted to see his daughter. He and Kelly had broken up and he was feeling "fatherly." Against my better judgment and the concerns of my family, I took my daughter to see him. There were bags and bags of clothes for her, toys, and souvenirs

And to YOU, Homeboy, I say "Thanks!"

from all the trips he took with Kelly and her children, Disney, Dorney park, etc. all the toys of which I donated to charity. The clothing, I kept. He claimed they were from his family even having his sister call me to tell me that, but I later found out from Kelly directly, that she had purchased them. When I confronted him with what Kelly said, he amended her statement with the word "stolen."
Oh well, I guess that whole credit card "thing" was TRUE. Damn her life was a mess.

Each weekend homeboy would be at my house, picking up his daughter for the weekend = four weekends in row and each time he showed up, he would need something = MONEY. Kalico Jones was now a published author and all over the internet, and in the book stores, so lend me, give me, can I have… would be the true focus of his visits, but being so desperate for my daughter to have a father, I did just that, gave, lent and spent.
I did everything in my power to facilitate a relationship between he and his daughter…EVERYTHING.

He was behind in support, I forgave the arrears. You see in the line of business he was in, the last thing he needed was for child support enforcement to garnish his wages and that's exactly what they threatened to do. I think once you get above a certain amount of unpaid child support the "system" begins to do things to you that hinder you from filing taxes, driving, etc. and so once homeboy got notice he was going to have "things" executed against his wages, license, etc. he felt the need to appeal to my "wanting" side, and showed up at my job.

"Mrs. Jones, you have a visitor."

"Its pretty early in the morning, Rita, would you happen to know the nature of the visit?"

"He says he's Ivy's dad Mrs. Jones."

"Okay you can send him up." I looked in the mirror. Don't ask me why. I guess I just wanted to make sure I looked good. But why? We were not together and so why should I care what he thought of my appearance. He opened the door to my office. "Good morning Miss Jones, you look nice."

"What's up Wiz, what are you doing here?"

"I needed to talk to you and I was in the area, so I stopped by...I called you first, but you didn't answer your phone."

"Oh, ok...what's up?"

"You see, I got this letter from the courts...(pulling out an envelope from his jacket pocket)...they are threatening to garnish my pay and suspend my license if I don't pay the back support in the amount of 12 thousand dollars."

I shook my head, "Okay and..." "And I don't have 12 thousand dollars and I can't get to work if I don't have a drivers license."

"Okay and...."

"And so I was wondering...I mean I had heard that you could just call the child support office and tell them that you are taking me off child support and they would not bother my license or job with a

And to YOU, Homeboy, I say "Thanks!"

garnishment."

"Wiz, I thought you and I agreed we were not going to have these kinds of conversations."

"I know, I know, but I need your help. If I can't drive then I can't see Ivy. You're not driving right now. What am I going to do?"

"Its what are YOU going to do? Are you going to pay your child support on time and in full once I do this? Are you going to help me out a little more with our daughter? What are you going to do?"

And right there sitting in my office, Homeboy solemnly promised to pay his child support every week, on time and in full. It sounded so sweet that if it didn't come out as smooth as butter, I would have thought his words were candy. (I'm laughing). And I guess he was laughing too 'cause guess what? Homeboy couldn't get out of my office building fast enough before I was on the phone with the courts executing the procedure to have the arrears forgiven…All 12 thousand dollars.

But it didn't stop there. He was behind in rent, I gave him the money, he needed a coat, I helped him out, clothing… a non issue = come by my job and get the money, over and over again.

Ring….ring….

"Hello"

"Kalico Jones, what's up baby, everyone is talking about your book"
(it was homeboy = baby daddy calling)

"Thanks, what's up with you?"

"I found a car and I want to know if you could help me with the down payment?"

And to YOU, Homeboy, I say "Thanks!"

"How much?"

"18 grand"

"18 grand, I don't have that kind of money!"

"No…that's how much the car is, I only need help with the
down payment."

"And how much money is help?"

"Three thousand" And I said, "yes" that's right, I was going to give
him the money, knowing I barely had enough for me and HIS
daughter to do things we needed to do sometimes. He came to my
house and got the check. The next day, after I confided in a family
member about the loan, I placed a stop payment on it.

On the phone with my cousin Susan…"What do you mean, you gave
this nigga three thousand dollars Kal?"

"He needed it for a car" "And your ass is driving a what again?…
Nothing! Bitch please, you better get your money back. This nigga is
playing games with you. I just saw him and Kelly last night laughing
and talking at the bar."

"Really?"

"Yes, really…and if you don't get your money back, I'm going to
tell your brothers and your mother!" I took a deep breath. Was this
nigga playing with my emotions? I am over him right? I'm just doing
this for my daughter right? Wrong… I wasn't truly over him. Shit…
That's when I called the bank and stopped payment on the check.
Shortly thereafter after I received several notices from the bank
regarding inquiries into my checking account, it was recommended

And to YOU, Homeboy, I say "Thanks!"

that I close the account.

Instead, I switched banks.
I guess he was pissed, because the very next week, I was served with court papers. He was taking me to court to get his child support payments lowered. He wasn't successful.

I could go on for days and days regarding things that have happened to me and who is truly at fault for the twists and turns life has taken me through. The drug abuse, the sexual assaults, rape, beatings, etc. but I will not. All I will say is I am I am free of the baby daddy drama, the drugs, the excessive drinking, abuse and the fake friends. Yes my friends I've been through it ALL, and IM STILL HERE.

I must admit it took me a long time to get to this point in my life where I am totally free of the bullshit. Free of going to bed at night thinking and wondering if Homeboy was going to come "save" me. Waking up and instead of thinking about selling books, going to work or enjoying the day God has blessed me with, I was stuck on whether or not Homeboy was thinking of me. If I truly held a special place in his heart, despite the drama. And after telling my story to just about anyone who would listen, a woman named June said to me, "Kalico you are in search of closure, my advice to you is write him a letter with everything you want to say in it, fold it nice and neat, drop it in a beer bottle and throw it in the gutter...he's bound to get it."

Damn that was harsh, but she was right. I needed closure and since his ass wasn't going to give it to me, I had to get it for myself.

And to YOU, Homeboy, I say "Thanks!"

I SAT DOWN AND WROTE THREE LETTERS FIRST UP...HOMEBOY

Dear Homeboy,

As I sit here attempting to deduce the occurrences of the past two years, I've slowly come to the conclusion that I am not nearly as over you as I once believed. I know this is not something that comes as a surprise to you because you have taken my very real and noticeable feelings and have manipulated your desires into my ACTIONS.

I look at you and still see a love strong enough to pull me from the streets. I look at you and see a man who despite my past, accepted me with open arms and protected me, but that is NOT who you are. I really can't figure out why I can only see the great things that once were when I look at you, especially since you've done so many things to me that were hurtful and with all due respect and acknowledgement, I to you as well. I never wanted to know the meaning of love and now I know why, because you never really get over your first love. You were my first love and our love helped bring forth the very person who will save my life, giving me something to truly focus on, other than...

I have tried so many times to reach out to you. To assist you with being a great part of your daughter's life, understanding the fact that an active father is essential in the life of a daughter. Its crazy though when I think back because I never thought I would be in this position, raising a child all by myself and I am not talking about the financial aspect of it because any mother of a child whose father is not around will say the same thing, "I would gladly give up the child support for time and attention for my child." And I have done just that. I have assisted you in more ways than I've assisted myself and our daughter on some occasions, and that's my harsh reality and something I have to deal with as I look back on the mistakes I have made with you. But the key phrase here is "look back" as I have no intention on bringing this into my future.

As a woman I feel that I would never date a man who did not take care of his children, in my defense, I don't think I ever did until now. As I go forward that will be my first question when meeting someone: "Do you have children and if so, are you active in their lives?" And being the person I am, I wouldn't be real if I didn't leave you with that very same question: "Are you active in your daughter's life?" The answer to that is "no" and the no is by choice because you've had so many opportunities to become involved. You have had more opportunities to be there for her, and over and over again, you choose not to and so I am choosing NOT to beg you for that any longer.

You are free to call or stop by if ever you wish to begin a real relationship with your daughter.
Take care of yourself!
The mother of your child

And I made a copy of it to put with all the other things that will allow me to fully explain what happened between me and homeboy, should

And to YOU, Homeboy, I say "Thanks!"

my daughter ever ask, "Mommy, where's my Daddy?" I mailed the original to him via express mail. I kept the receipt to prove it.

I began to realize I had power over my emotions and that he didn't deserve my love or hurt for that matter. And truth be told, if he didn't want to be bothered with his daughter, then it wasn't for me to continue to try and force him or his family to be in her life. It was and will remain, MY responsibility to ensure the health and well-being of my daughter and having been through so much in my life, this too was just another hurdle I was going to have to accept and jump over in order to really be free.

MY NEXT LETTER WENT TO HIS SISTER A CORRECTION OFFICE IN PHILADELPHIA

I was going to call LaToya at first, but then I thought a letter would probably be best. I could get my point across without being interrupted and she could soak in everything I said without having the pressure of responding.

LaToya,

I wanted to write you sooner or give you a call, but I decided to wait until after the dust settled from my criminal trials, the custody battle, etc.

Just to let you know, all charges alleged against me by Kelly have been dropped due to lack of evidence and participation on behalf of the complaining witness and as far as the custody battle…I have sole legal, physical custody of our daughter.

But that is NOT what I would like to talk about in this letter. Listen LaToya, your brother and I clearly did not handle the break up between us as adults. We have collectively destroyed whatever we could have had, but Ivy should not be excluded from her family because of it.

I send you guys pictures, invitations to birthday parties and other celebrations and the invitations and calls are not responded to. You have told me that no matter what, you would stay out of it. I didn't

And to YOU, Homeboy, I say "Thanks!"

think that by staying out of "it" you meant my daughters LIFE, At least not at the time in which you said it.

I guess what I am saying is that, I have reached my limit with your brother and have truly given up on him ever being an active part in his daughters life, but that doesn't have anything to do with you, your mom and the rest of your family. I am asking for you to please remember you have a niece out here in Jersey.

I hope things are going well with you. I have changed our home phone numbers and Ivy has her own cell phone, you can always call her direct. Well, take care and tell your daughter I said hello, I'm sure she's grown into a sweet young lady.

Respectfully, Kali

I hand wrote our new telephone number, along with Ivy's cell phone number on the letter, made a copy and expressed mailed it to Philadelphia. I kept the receipt for my records as well.

TWO DOWN ONE TO GO
NEXT UP...HIS MOMMA

Dear Charlotte,

I am writing you this letter in hopes you will respond this time. A question for you, if I may...What is it that I have done to you that would make you respond to my actions, by being a no show in the life of your grand-daughter? Ivy has called you so many times and you have yet to respond. She has sent you Holiday cards, gifts and photos and never once have you telephoned or written to say "Thank you" or to acknowledge receipt. Your actions and the actions of your family lead me to wonder if there is anything I have done to upset you, personally. If there is something I have done, well let me take this time to apologize, as it is never my intent to hurt anyone, but as a mother it is my instinct and God given duty to do whatever is necessary to protect my child and so if your feelings stem from something in that area, the apology stands, but I would hope that you would UNDERSTAND my position, as a parent.

It's becoming increasing clear, unfortunately, that your son's role in his daughter's life is not one that he finds necessary at this point in HIS life. Hopefully that will change, but to be quite honest, I don't foresee that happening. Although I have come to the hurtful conclusion that your family may never include Ivy as your own, I will not hinder any

And to YOU, Homeboy, I say "Thanks!"

communication between you and her, but as of today…I will not longer
ENCOURAGE it.

There is no reason a child should have to beg an adult for love, especially
when the adults consist of: a father, a grandmother and a host of aunts,
uncles and cousins. Today I discontinue "selling" my daughter as though
she is a used car to her family. As her mother I can no longer do this and
as a seasoned parent, I know you would not expect me to.
As I have explained to your daughter and your son, if you would like
to contact Ivy, I will never object, but if its not going to be with any
regularity, then I would ask that you continue to refrain from contacting
her until your life permits you to be consistent.

I wish you well. Respectfully,
K. Jones
Those letters were mailed out four months ago…

We haven't heard from homeboy since.

Or his sister

Or his mother.

My daughter is the only person in this mess whose behavior has been 100 percent consistent. She loves everyone in her family and constantly asks about and for them. We continue to send cards, gifts and photos and she gets NOTHING. Not even a call on her birthday from any of them, including her father. How REAL is that?

But in the midst of all this. This fucked up drama that is my life, I refuse to allow people to force me to act out of character. I continue to grow as a person, and a parent I am doing "my thing!" Now don't get me wrong, I have moments of weakness where I want to call Homeboy and ask him just what in the hell is going on in his life where he feels as though being an active parent is unnecessary and just when I pick up the phone to dial his number, I remember...

I DON'T HAVE IT.

So what's up with me now? Well I haven't been high since the day my mother and brothers gave me that surprise visit in the Bronx... and that was five years ago.

And I owe it all to Homeboy, "Thanks Homeboy!" Kalico was single, drug free (again) and going to love it. I dressed myself up and took my black ass out on the town.

And to YOU, Homeboy, I say "Thanks!"

3 MONTHS AFTER MY "DISCOVER OF THYSELF" I MET MR. RIGHT

Here comes Kevin…

I love Kevin, we are good in bed, good in conversation, good with our children, and good looking. We've got it going on. In the two years we've been dating, we've meshed our families and we lived as one big happy family. Kevin is attentive, he notices everything. Buys me nice gifts and for NO reason at all. I just come home to gifts for me and my daughter. He spoils us and I love it.

I met Kevin at a rap concert. He managed one of the performing artists. I was backstage doing an on the spot interview for a local cable TV show.

Trying to get through the crowd of groupies, the homeboys that accompanied the rap artists, the press, there was me…in everybody's way, clutching my purse in one hand and my press pass in the other. "Excuse me, excuse me…(tapping the shoulder of a very good looking, tall man with a nice build), I'm Kalico Jones, the cable show sent me to interview Spiro."
Looking down in a "who said that" kind of way, the man whose

shoulder I tapped discovers me in the midst of what seemed like a thousand people, waving my arms above the crowd while yelling, "I'm over here!"

"Did you say you were Kalico Jones? We were expecting you, come on through" and he led me through the crowd. I wiped my face, "Thank you sir…ugh…this scene sure has changed, it was nothing like this when I was out there."

"Yeah, it's a whole new breed of bitches now…they are ruthless and will do anything for nothing, I'm glad I only have boys."

"Yeah well I have a daughter and I would be lying if I said I am not afraid for her when she grows up."

We smiled and he went into this private room where someone from BET was interviewing Spiro. I had to wait my turn, which wasn't so bad because I was in what I considered to be "good company."

"Oh, I'm sorry, where are my manners, my name is Kevin Planter, I am Spiro's manager. I also manage six other artists."

"Really"

"Yeah really."

"Anyone I've every heard of?"

"No, they aren't out yet…but we're in the studio. I've got artist development deals with Puff Lite and I'm meeting with Hov next week to talk about this R&B chick outta Harlem I want to put on the team."

Now I know who Puff Lite and Hov are, but aside from the few people I jayed (screwed) over the years in the industry, I didn't know shit about artist development deals, etc. and so I believed Kevin. I mean he was here with Spiro, representing him as his manager, so why would he lie, right?

After my interview with Spiro, Kevin and I exchanged numbers. I told him where I was living and he responded with, "Oh I just brought a few buildings there and I have a house not too far from where you live, how are you getting home?"
"The 66 Bus out of port authority, why…you giving me a ride?"
"No I left my Bentley down south. I had to fly back for an emergency and I haven't had the chance to go get it…but I have no problem with you getting in a taxi with me if you don't feel like riding the bus, since I am going that way."

Well I was not about to front like I enjoyed taking the bus, 'cause I did not. I accepted the offer. When the event was completely over and Kevin said goodnight to his artist, we walked out of the venue and across the street to Niles, a nice little restaurant on Seventh Avenue, for a late supper before hailing a taxi back to Jersey. Dinner was great.
Kevin told me stories about his run ins with everyone in the music industry from Sugar Cane the Don to Young Jesus and MC Spitz… He knew more people than me or so I thought. And just when I thought the conversation was going good, a little one-side, but entertaining, he asked me about me!

And to YOU, Homeboy, I say "Thanks!"

Damn...Do I tell him about the book? Do I tell him that I've been with more men than he's probably been with women...and do I mention the women too? I decided to keep the conversation about me short, "I'm a freelance writer, self published author and single parent of one little girl. I'm from Mt. Vernon but I never really hung out there once I realized there was life outside of that town. I spent most of my time partying in Harlem, deep downtown NYC, North Carolina, Vegas, California and I just recently moved to New Jersey. And just so you don't ask, NO I don't get along with my daughter's father which is not a problem being as he doesn't even check on his daughter at all." And as I was giving Kevin the "standard definition" of "who is Kalico Jones" his cell phone rang.

He excused himself from the table. But for what? I could still hear him talking. Shit he was so loud I'm sure everyone in the restaurant heard him. He was yelling and screaming and then at the end of his conversation, he said, Fuck you Puff Lite!" and hung up the phone. When he returned to the table, I didn't say word about what I and the rest of the patrons at Niles heard.

"So where were we?" I said as I gulped down my glass of wine.

"Sorry about that...its just that people tend to forget who gave them their first business loan..." and he went on and on about helping Puff Lite out when he was down.

And I'm thinking to myself, "When was Puff Lite ever down?" Ok well again that's none of my business. I just wanted to get home. My daughter was with Shayna, my office helper slash "ninth inning"

And to YOU, Homeboy, I say "Thanks!"

sitter and she was a party animal, so I had to make sure I was home by midnight so she could do her usual run around.

We didn't talk much during dinner after that. It was just Kevin making a bunch of calls, talking loud and being just him, I guess. I didn't make much of it. I figured that's the nature of the business, especially when you are managing artists. I don't know, you see the music industry was never anything I was interested in.

And to YOU, Homeboy, I say "Thanks!"

CHECK PLEASE!

It was almost midnight and I expressed my need to be home soon to Kevin, who politely called the waiter over for the check and we exited the restaurant.

Belly full and feeling a little sleepy...I put my head on his shoulder and fell asleep. He woke me up at the Grove Street exit off Route 3 West. "Kalico...Kalico...time to get up...I don't know exactly where you live and so you have to direct the driver from here."

Rubbing my eyes and checking my breath before I spoke...hey... first impressions...I directed the taxi driver to my apartment and thanked Kevin for his generosity with regards to the dinner and ride home, as I offered to leave the tip.

"I don't want your money...I want to see you again, can I have your number?"

"I gave it to you already, remember?"

"I don't want THAT number...I want your home number. I want the number to that right there," as he pointed up to my second floor apartment window.

I handed him a piece of paper with my home telephone number on it and he pointed out one of the buildings he owned...directly across the street from my house. Damn! This is too close for comfort, but it's ok.

 The 2nd Installment of the Kalico Jones Trilogy

7AM

Ring…ring…

ring….ring….

"Hello"

"What's up baby…are you still sleeping?"

"Who IS this?"

"This is Kevin…I want to take you and your daughter to breakfast. Be ready at 10, I'm coming to get you guys."

"I don't introduce my daughter to people like that Kevin. Maybe one day down the road you can meet her, but me and her father's breakup is still fresh for both of us and they are not close and I don't want her to get used to another man until her father gets his shit together. I know you understand."

"No I don't understand. Does he know he has a daughter?"

"Of course, that's a dumb question, yes…he knows."

"Then he has no excuse. You showed me a photo of her last night. She is beautiful. If he is not interested in her, don't hinder someone else from being a father figure or a friend. That's not right."

I took a deep breath. Was Kevin right? "Well, ok" and reluctantly I allowed Kevin to take me and my daughter out to breakfast. And

And to YOU, Homeboy, I say "Thanks!"

from then on the three of us were inseparable. This guy was Mr. Absolutely Right. There was no doubt in my mind he was the one.

Great sex, great conversation. If I was running late from signings or events, he would get my daughter off the school bus. They would go out together. Do father / daughter things. I thought it was going to be just us. His children were adorable too. Two boys, both of whom I thought the world of. But there was some stuff about Kevin that I found to be odd. Some things he said just didn't match up with things members of his family told me. All things that were basically in surrounding material possessions and so I could get beyond that. I went to him one day after dating for six months, "Kevin…I want to give you my six month opportunity."

"What's that?"

"If there is anything you have not been completely honest with me about, you can come clean now and get a 'pass' which means I will not hold it against you or make mention of it ever. Now if you feel you can't tell me that you have lied to me about something…please just don't ever lie to me again. There is nothing you can't tell me, you do know that right?"

"Of course I know that Pookie. And there is nothing you have to worry about. I have not lied to you. There is nothing I need a 'pass' for…stop punishing me for the things that happened between you and your ex, its not fair. And besides, I thought we were beyond that now."

And to YOU, Homeboy, I say "Thanks!"

AND GUESS WHAT?
WE WERE BEYOND THAT SO I
BELIEVED HIM
I TOOK HIM AT HIS WORD
AND 8 MONTHS LATER

It all came back to bite me in the ass.

The buildings…

NOT his.

The house in Florida…

NOT his.

There was NO Bentley, which would explain why when I inquired as to when I would get the chance to see a real Bentley up close, he replied with, "Pookie, I told you it was stolen. Don't you remember?"

Of course I didn't remember and how could I? He never told me no shit like that. Who would forget a stolen Bentley story. But that's not the end of it… There were no Artist development deals. Shit Puff Lite didn't even know who he was, let alone Hov. He told me he was working at Werner Bros. That was a lie as well. I didn't confront Kevin right away with my findings. I loved him so. And more than that… my daughter loved him and so the last thing I wanted to do was hurt her in the process of dumping him. I made a choice to stick it out with him. I mean he did treat me and my daughter good so, what's

And to YOU, Homeboy, I say "Thanks!"

the big deal, right? Wrong! Each day Kevin came home with a story about how his day at Werner Bros went. He just signed "this" artist or "that" singer…it was ALWAYS some story about how successful his day was. And that would be fine, if it really happened, but I knew it didn't. And I knew eventually my feelings for him would change, and they did. I felt betrayed. I mean he read the books (When Gucci Came First, and its follow up – And to you Homeboy I say thanks). He saw the interaction between me and Homeboy first hand. He was there when the shit hit the fan between me and members of my family. He was there to hold my hand through all that. When the panic attacks came back…The excessive drinking…The cigarettes (ugh…I'm sucking my teeth) Who do you think rocked with me through all those things? KEVIN did because I had NO ONE in my corner at that time…NO ONE! I knew he cared for me and so I'm thinking that maybe he felt as though he had to continue to lie because that's how he started off with me. I began to resent the fact that my six month "pass" didn't mean shit to him and it showed. I tried to think of how I would break the news to my daughter. I really didn't want to tell her what was going on. She's just a kid. She's got enough things to deal with like learning the alphabet, how to spell and write. This is why I was against having them meet in the first place. I mean this would be man number two out of her life. First her father and now after two years of being with Kevin…HIM!

        The 2nd Installment of the Kalico Jones Trilogy

And to YOU, Homeboy, I say "Thanks!"

I PICKED UP THE PHONE
AND CALLED PUDDA

Who subsequently is the only person I keep in contact from my old hometown with any regularity. But that could be because she hasn't lived there in years either.

Ring…ring…

Ring…ring…

"Hello"

"Hey Pudda, this is Kalico, are you busy?"

"What's up girl, you need to talk?"

"Yeah…I could really use your ability to not pass judgment right about now."

"You know I won't…what's up?"

"Remember when we talked about trust and all that good stuff you look for in a man?"

"Yeah, you said that you were having strong feelings for Kevin"

"And you said…"

"And I said, I didn't think it was a good idea to continue the relationship because there were too many discrepancies in his stories to you."

"Yeah, that conversation…well girl I wish I had taken your advice and ended it then."

And to YOU, Homeboy, I say "Thanks!"

"Why Kal what happened?"

"I wouldn't know where to begin. First of all the buildings… NOT his."

"Which would explain why he's been at your house for two months now…renovations, my ass. Nothing takes that long when you've got money."

"But hold on…there's more…NO Bentley."

"I could have told you that. A nigga with a Bentley he doesn't show off? Yeah right. Okay so that's two things."

"There's more…the job at Werner Bros. Non existent. And the other day I met his younger son's mother and he introduced me as 'Kalico Jones, the girl who wrote the book I gave you for Christmas."

"Oh no he didn't?"

"Yes, he did. And to top that off, she spent the night. He claims they didn't sleep together. He slept on the sofa."

"I knew I didn't like him for a reason."

"But it gets better than that, I went to the apartment and saw used condoms in the garbage."

"Now girl I know your ass ain't going through this nigga's garbage can."

Laughing, "No…I didn't go through his garbage. My daughter dropped a piece of candy on the floor, I picked it up, went to throw it in the garbage, looked down and saw the condoms. When I questioned him about it, he said that since he is at my place all the time, he let his Uncle use the apartment and that more than likely the condom belonged to his uncle."

And to YOU, Homeboy, I say "Thanks!"

"Kalico Jones, I know you didn't fall for that? I just know you didn't!"

"Pudda, you said you weren't going to pass judgment."

"You mean the judgment you're not using, judgment!"

I exhaled, "I know, I'm fucking up on this. Its like my senses are off. In my defense, I haven't dated in a LONG time. Since homeboy really. Maybe I'm not as ready as I thought I was."

"And you're just figuring that out? Everyone around you can tell you're not ready for a relationship, let alone a serious relationship."

"Don't say that, that's not right."

"It doesn't have to be right when its REAL. You can't go one day without talking about Homeboy. How good the relationship was in the beginning. How you guys had everything. How you wish you could turn back time. Blah blah blah…"

"What's that suppose to mean?"

"It means you are NOT over him. You needed more time to put your heart back together before you jumped into a relationship with this lying asshole. You've focused on being a mother to the point where you barely go out. We can't even have a decent girl's night out without you making some excuse to leave early and you've gained a few pounds around the middle. I'm trying to figure out just what you are trying to prove by being homely."

"Homely. I dress nice. I have my hair, my nails, my full face of make up when I roll out. Yeah, I may have gained a little weight, but I'm still good…men try to talk to me all day every day."

"And some of those men would have been good for you, but you chose this retard and now we have to deprogram your daughter."

"I know…I don't know what I am going to do. She loves him and I think I do too."

"You love your daughter's father. You love your daughter…you love to shop and spend money…you do NOT love Kevin. It was just something for you to do to prevent your ass from being alone, but there is a BIG difference between being ALONE and LONELY. And you, my friend were NOT alone. You were lonely and so you made a not so good decision."

"Damn, I'm going to miss all the presents."

"You need to be wondering where his ass is all day when he is supposed to be a job he doesn't really have."

I heard the door open. It was Kevin coming in the house, "Pudda, I'm going to call you back."

"Oh he must be there…Kal, cut that nigga off today. Get it over with."

"Ok, I'm gone."

"Call me tomorrow from work."

"Okay." I hung up the phone, walked to the door, and asked Kevin a question, "Have I ever done anything to you or maybe said something to you that made you think you could not be honest with me?"

"Of course not Pookie, why do you ask?"

"No reason really…I just wanted to give you another chance to lie to me before I cut you off. We're over…my house keys please…and don't ever think about calling me after this!"

Why did I cut him off just like that you ask? Because I gave him

And to YOU, Homeboy, I say "Thanks!"

chance after chance to be honest and he continuously refused. And to top that off, he read my books, and I remember one day being told by a close friend, "Kalico if anyone can read When Gucci Came First and know that most of that story about you is true and STILL lie and hurt you…they don't deserve to know you."

And she was right.

And so ends that encounter.

The funny shit about the entire thing is that he is such a nice person and I enjoyed him so much, that he could have picked garbage for a living for all I cared. He was just that sweet. (taking a deep breath) I should have seen the signs early on with Kevin's ass. He was a loud talker and my "saying" about loud talkers is simple: Loud talker, listen LESS!

And my daughter…well she's handling the breakup well. She does Kevin the same way she now does her father…NEVER ASK ABOUT HIM. What I've noticed is that one Toys R Us shopping spree will deprogram any four year old.

Thank Goodness!

And NO one is meeting my daughter in that capacity again. You figure she's four and have met TWO men who are not around. So let's do that math. Two men in four years. That's one man per two years. At that rate, by the time she turns eight, she could meet four men, then by ten five men and by twenty…possible TEN men…All of whom would not be in her life. Mommy the "ho!"

I don't think so.

And to YOU, Homeboy, I say "Thanks!"

I've been there, done that and I am not going to revisit that life in my mid thirties and being a mother. Its back to getting to "know thyself" again.

Since the break up Kevin has moved back to New York City and I've only seen him about three or four times. He's living in Harlem in an apartment he had the entire time we dated. I guess that's where he was during the day when he was supposed to be at work. And get this…he finally got a job in the music industry. I saw him in a music video with one of his artists last week on 106 & Park.

Oh well.

     The 2nd Installment of the Kalico Jones Trilogy

And to YOU, Homeboy, I say "Thanks!"

JUST WHEN YOU THINK IT'S SAFE TO GO BACK IN THE WATER... HERE COMES THAT MUSIC AGAIN

December 22,

Ring…Ring..

Ring.. ring…

I noticed my daughter's father number on the caller Id. I took a deep breath and answered the phone. We have been getting along lately, but then again…we barely speak when he calls.

I answered the phone, "Hey what's up"

"Nothing, what's my little girl doing?"

"She's over here crying."

"Why?"

"Because I told her that Santa was going to come and take all the gifts back if she doesn't clean her room."

"Kal you know I don't like that Santa fantasy, put her on the phone."

And I did just that. I handed my daughter the telephone so she could speak with her daddy, of whom I haven't fought with in over three months, good. We're speaking again and so subconsciously I interpreted the "calmness" and speaking terms for "caring" yet again. After about thirty minutes of her speaking with her father. She passed the phone back to me.

"Kal I have to tell you something."

My heart skipped a beat, could this be the moment where he realizes he still loves me and wants to come back home? "What's up?"

He sighed and said, "I have a confession to make."

I felt myself getting warm. I began to perspire…Oh my goodness, he's going to do it. He's going to tell me he's sorry and we're going to move on and be together again as a family…Thank you Jesus, thank you God…Ok Kal, calm down, don't rush to judgment. But what else could it be? I love him, I know he loves me…what could it be?

He continued, "KJ, I have a girlfriend who I love very much and my mother likes her too."

NO he didn't!

Ok KJ try to keep your composure. Stay dignified…keep calm, don't say shit…its ok and you're going to be ok. Stay dignified…keep calm, don't say shit…its ok and you're going to be ok…. I felt my hand shake. I began to whisper to myself… "Don't drop the phone, remain calm, you're ok…don't drop the phone, remain calm, you're ok."

It took all the strength I had left in me not to flip the fuck out. I wanted to lose control. I felt myself getting ready to ask his ass what in the hell was he thinking coming at me like that and why is it that he always shows his ass around the holidays. Why? Why? Why?

I responded, "That's wonderful, she must be nice, that's wonderful."

– LYING

"Yeah, she's great. And she loves our daughter."

"They met?"

"Yeah, she is the girl who was in the car when me and my aunt picked our daughter up that weekend."

"I thought that was your cousin's girlfriend."

"No she was with me."

His aunt is a fucking liar. She clearly stated to me the girl in attendance was with HER son…Bitch! And if they were so "together," why didn't he introduce her to me. I mean she was going to be spending time with MY daughter. Well I was not going to front like I was happy for him, because I was NOT. I was pissed! Pulling this shit on me a few days before Christmas, can I get a fucking break? I know we've been getting along = speaking, for a few months, but we are not by a long shot…FRIENDS.

I have been the Easter Bunny, the Tooth Fairy, Mommy the trick or treater, and I have done everything by MYSELF and now that it's Christmas, my black ass has to be Santa Claus…or so I thought because during his conversation with our daughter, he told her Santa wasn't real.

Bastard!

So I guess this is the part when I say I can't stand his ass, but I am not. There was a lot of love between Homeboy and me and although

And to YOU, Homeboy, I say "Thanks!"

its official…ITS over, I am not going to take it there.

I had to ask myself a question: Why in the fuck would you want someone who doesn't fucking help you? Why would you want someone who doesn't even call to check up on their own child? Why would you want to deal with a family who has literally abandoned a little girl for what is now going on FIVE, count 'em, FIVE fucking years? Why? What is wrong with YOU KJ? Why would you allow yourself to be so effected by someone who has shown you on more occasions than you would like to admit, they have NO love for you, no respect and only love your child when its convenient. When did you become a fucking punk?

I think in my attempt to change my life I have allowed people to say and do shit to me that under other circumstances, I would have slapped the shit out of them. And my daughter's father's behavior is an example of how I have allowed things to spin out of control. I guess the saying, "Be careful what you pray for is true."

       The 2nd Installment of the Kalico Jones Trilogy

And to YOU, Homeboy, I say "Thanks!"

MY PRAYER TO GOD JUST 2 DAYS PRIOR TO HOMEBOY'S "Confessional" PHONE CALL

"Hey God, what's up…its me. I am coming to you today because I've been through the mill this year and I just need closure on so many things, especially my daughter's father. I need closure because despite one day possibly finding someone who will really love me and my daughter, I'm afraid I won't be able to give myself to him because I am still in love with my daughters father. I know it's been some time now, almost five years, but he was the one who encouraged me and stood by me when NO one else did. He stuck by me when attacks against my character were at an all time high and I know his purpose in my life has probably been served in your eyes, but I love him and if there is no chance of us ever being together, please do something to release me from him emotionally so I can move on once and for all. I have many other things to say, but I will save those items for another time. Thanks for looking out. In Jesus name I pray. Amen"

And so now it was time for me to finally release myself emotionally from the person who has released himself emotionally from me.

Brian McKnight "Last Cry" playing in the background… "One last cry…before I leave it all behind…I've got to put you out of my mind…I guess I'm down to my last cry…"

(Exhaling) I wish him well.

I realized after trying ALL the rest, its time for me to try the BEST.

And to YOU, Homeboy, I say "Thanks!"

The only man for me right now is Jesus. He is my lover, my protector, the father of my child and very...**necessary.**

Reaching outside of the divine order has set me back a bit. Being a mother before a wife, being a friend to others before being a friend to myself. Using champagne, cigarettes, and cocaine to self medicate me from my reality...yeah, I can say it's been a story to tell to say the very least. Since the phone call from Homeboy, my daughter has not heard from her father. We have not gotten a response from his family or a thank you for that matter, for the gifts, cards and photos we've sent over the years. During a conversation with my daughter a few weeks back, I almost explained to her the meaning of "deadbeat" – but the damage potential far out weighed the need for me to keep it real with a five year old. I figured she would soon be old enough to develop her own opinion of her father, until then...he will always be the GREATEST DAD ON EARTH.

I'm focused and single by choice. I don't smoke or get high, and the drinking...well it's no longer excessive and as far as being a single parent...I'm great at it and I OWE it all to homeboy.

Thanks Homeboy!

I always told people he "broke my heart" until I realized, it wasn't whole in the first place.

And that my friend is the end of my story. Thanks for listening.

"The thing you fear most has no power. Your fear of it is what has the power. Facing the truth really will set you free."
-Oprah Winfrey

<h2 style="text-align:center">And to YOU, Homeboy, I say "Thanks!"</h2>

Where are they now?(The Major Characters from When Gucci Came First)

My mother... When I do signings and speaking engagements I am always asked about the relationship between me and my mother, so I will say this to clear the air...my mother and I are cool peeps. I think we are more "buddies" than mother / daughter sometimes, but she is great at being a Grandmother and me and my daughter love her very much. We've had issues, but they are in the past. I am confident our relationship will continue to grow. **My brothers Joey and Charlie** are the same. ...they both have great jobs and continue to be great fathers to their children and role models to others. **My father** is doing just fine and yes, he is still a pastor in North Carolina. **Hev from Brooklyn** and I are in contact with each other. He owns a club in lower Manhattan and is still keeps a revolving door when it comes to women. **Mr. Moore** and I are still contact. He is in the final stage of his incarceration ...No comment on whether or not we are married. **Mr. Diamond Bracelet** and I are STILL friends, he's a huge part of my past and responsible for most of the good times. I can't go into his whereabouts, but rest assure, I see him a few times a year under the cover of darkness for "federal" reasons. **Mr. Realtor,** still calls me every year on my birthday. **Mr. NBA** is no longer playing professionally. I really don't know how he is and personally I don't care. **Mrs. Mattress Tester from Hempstead a.k.a Nettie** is somewhere in the Bronx. As far as her and I speaking, that will never happen. I'm sure her and homeboy are still in contact, if not, then the fuck was truly NOT worth it. **Monet** and I are sisters for life, I don't see her much, and we don't talk often but when we do, it's a great conversation, and yeah... I still owe her the 100 bucks. **Russ** is married to the woman he was dating when he and I were seeing each other, and GOOD for him! **Mr. GTI** is in jail from my understanding and unfortunately the third party of our "threesome" **Five – Two (really 25)** passed away a few months ago on my birthday. Oh and I never saw **Kelly** again. **Or her father.**

*****WHEN GUCCI CAME FIRST, 10 YEARS IN THE GAME...REMIX COMING SOON*********2009

And to YOU, Homeboy, I say "Thanks!"
ACKNOWLEDGEMENTS

A Psalm of David. To thee, O LORD, I call; my rock, be not deaf to me, lest, if thou be silent to me, I become like those who go down to the Pit. Hear the voice of my supplication, as I cry to thee for help, as I lift up my hands toward thy most holy sanctuary. Take me not off with the wicked, with those who are workers of evil, who speak peace with their neighbors, while mischief is in their hearts. Requite them according to their work, and according to the evil of their deeds; requite them according to the work of their hands; render them their due reward ..Blessed be the LORD! for he has heard the voice of my supplications. The LORD is my strength and my shield; in him my heart trusts; so I am helped, and with my song I give thanks to him.

A Special "Thanks" to Whom? "Thank you Jesus, for sustaining and confirming me every day. You allow me to wakeup every morning because I have not finished the mission and various assignments you need me to fulfill." **Thank you to all those who I consider "Family"**

Translation: Thanks to those who I love and respect and those who love and respect me & my daughter.

And in the words of my Father, the Pastor… "Jesus loves you and so do I…bye, bye, bye, bye, bye."

Wanna write me? Kalicojones@yahoo.com Feel free to write a review on amazon.com and barnesandnoble.com. Thank you for your support!

www.thekalicojonesproject.com come check out what I'm up to!

And to YOU, Homeboy, I say "Thanks!"

Other books by Kalico Jones
EXCERPTS

WHEN GUCCI CAME FIRST
True Tales of a Tramp

And so your journey begins...

Last night, I was out with this guy "Q." He's a fellow PK (preacher's kid) at a bar in New Jersey. After having several drinks "Q" invited me back to his apartment. He said he had access to some good cocaine and since I hadn't seen him in a while I agreed to keep him company.

We walked two blocks from the bar to the apartment he shared with a friend who worked nights. Upon our arrival, "Q" told me that he had to go upstairs to get the "stuff" from a dealer who just happened to live in the building.

He returned 45 minutes later...

When "Q" re-entered the room. I immediately asked him how much my portion of the tab was. His response, "Nah Diamond, I got it." Now although my dear friend "Q" had offered to pay for our party favors, I didn't want him to think I owed him a "favor," so I gave him half the money he spent at his neighbor's house, $55.00.

    The 2nd Installment of the Kalico Jones Trilogy

And to YOU, Homeboy, I say "Thanks!"

I opened the little plastic baggie and scooped out some of an off-white, really close to yellow substance that was just passed off to me as cocaine and took a hit. Twice up each nostril. My nose froze immediately. I sucked my teeth and said, "There's too much cut on this shit…I can't sniff this crap, shit!" So pissed, having paid $55.00 for garbage, I grabbed a glass, filled it with Bacardi, dropped in two pieces of ice and decided to get drunk instead. But there was one problem, I started feeling high. I thought, "Damn, I hate being high off beat." I sat back on "Q's" bed, smoked a cigarette and waited for my high to come down.

30 minutes later...

My high was gone but my dear friend "Q" was just getting started. He was in the corner of his room (in front of the window, no less), rolling up a dollar bill like a straw. He snorted three lines of cocaine off the top of his dresser. I was flabbergasted and apparently that wasn't enough, because he then poured the little bit of cocaine left in the bag I had in a pipe and lit it!

Oh my goodness, he's a fucking CRACK HEAD! I gotta get the fuck out of here quick. I asked him to walk me back to the bar and he responded with, "Can I have a kiss?"

You should've seen the look on my face, utterly disgusted at this point (I just wasted $55.00 on bullshit, I can't get drunk and now he blows the little bit of high I had with this stupid ass question). "Sorry 'Q' but I don't do anything buzzed." He started laughing and took another hit of his dirty ass pipe. To this day, I have never seen a person suck up smoke the way he did. I know the pipe LOOKED dirty, but was it clogged too? Damn, he needs help. He blew the smoke towards my face and replied in a Jamaican accent, "I respect that."

Yeah right...now you know his ass was lying.

"Can we please leave?" I said, as I felt it necessary to ask his ass a SECOND time, to walk me back to the bar. I put on my jacket and told him I was leaving. He said he needed to change his shirt (that took fifteen minutes). He then tried on several suit jackets (another ten minutes) and finally at 1:15am, we were on our way out the door. The bar was closed.

I walked home by myself in the freezing cold, clutching a torn piece of paper with his number on it.

I looked down at his number and thought, "I hope he doesn't expect to hear from me tomorrow." As a matter of fact, I hope he doesn't expect to hear from me ever again, fuckin' CRACK HEAD!

I know, I know, how can I call him a crack head, right?

Listen...I have a weird perception of people who do cocaine. I guess it's because I don't consider myself an addict, and that whole crack pipe, smoking coke thing seems so offensively "fiendish" to me (if that's a word). I feel like this: if you sniff it, that's okay, a rich mans high and as long as you can afford it, you DO NOT HAVE A PROBLEM. Now, if you SMOKE it, you're a fiend, period!

I guess my mindset on this is largely due to the fact that one of the TVs in my home was purchased from a pipe-smoking fiend. It's a sick

And to YOU, Homeboy, I say "Thanks!"

justification, I know, but as you will see, I've developed many sick justifications over the years.

When I'm not doing cocaine, I have a drink in my hand. I know it's substitution and you better not say shit to me about it, 'cause if you do, I'm gonna say, "At least I'm not getting high!" and I might tell you to go fuck yourself (depending on how many drinks I've had), so mind your fuckin' business!

KJ THREE SIX FIVE (The Diary Vol. 1)

Daily entries taken directly from my site and published, at the advice of my readers.

08/19 - Hello all...today's reflections are a product of family circumstances. I mention the truth shall set you free...so I will say this: What good is keeping "the peace" when the peace is phony? It's your place to demand respect from others and family is no exception. When difficulties arise, get your point across and don't waive your feelings for the sake of keeping peace. You'll only harbor resentment. -kJ

And to YOU, Homeboy, I say "Thanks!"

08/31 -Or what I like to call, "The Final Day of Summer" School shopping, looking for a new place to live - possibly a relocation, and completing my second book. I'm tired, I've got some things going on and I just deleted myself from the long list of Authors groups I belonged to. No reason to explain, just I feel at this time I do not need to be part of a clique to advance in publishing. I feel as though the streets are my reviewers, so no thanks on that. I'm not trying to be funny, I don't think I'm better than others...but lets face it. I'm FROM the streets and so that's who I let judge me. Kalico send us 9 copies of your book for review? NO. Kalico we would like to add you to our web page, just let us review your book, and by the way...we need 4 copies. NO thanks. I will continue to let the streets handle my book sales, and reviews, your help is not necessary at this time. Publishing to me is a business! I'm not here to make friends with everyone who comes across my path. I'm just here to make a difference. I'm sure you can understand that. **So today I say, Blaze your OWN trail. Be your OWN judge and don't let anyone dictate your life to you! peace! KJ.**

09/01- Today's topic. When enough is ENOUGH!
You have friends, you have family, you have associates, all out for one thing, Your time. But when do you begin to put a dollar amount = value on YOUR time? When does your time become valuable to you? I have come to the conclusion - just for today, of course - that my time is VALUABLE and therefore should not be wasted. Don't waste my time. You need something, ask, get it and move on. Don't

expect me to babysit you. don't expect me to allow you to reach your goals via my time. I've got my own goals. So any time I take out for you is time taken away from me. So please if someone is nice enough to help you, learn whatever it is they are doing for you, so you can do it for yourself. Don't be a time waster. - KJ.

09/03-Well today I will be traveling, actually for the next week I am traveling. Going South. Maybe find a home for my family and me. Check out the book stores in the area, been getting a lot of country love re: When Gucci Came First, so you know a sista gots to go around and check in on those who have supported me. Introduce them to the new books - that's right, BOOKS, plural and just relax. Tried to have a conversation with baby daddy this morning, too bad it didn't go as planned. Ok see this is why ladies WE have got to do "it" for ourselves. WE have to be independent of the b.s. Life is better for you when you treat baby daddy like a business transaction. Damn shame I have to say this, but you know your girl Kal, she's gonna be real...If he ain't going to give your child the love and respect and most Important, TIME...then make sure your child gets the money. **Don't try to force him to do what he should feel in his heart. Always keeping it real, KJ over and OUT!**

9/13 - The day after the weekend it stormed... I can't even tell you guys how this weekend has made me stop and think, "When did Kalico become a punk?" First, my car was Impounded, yes, Impounded and I was given five tickets two of them court appearances, then I had

And to YOU, Homeboy, I say "Thanks!"

drama with baby daddy You see, unfortunate for him, he didn't enlist what I like to call, **CONSEQUENTIAL THINKING.** It's when you think about the consequences of your actions frame by frame prior to acting on dumb ass Impulses. You have to evaluate how your irrational behavior is going to affect the overall relationships (you and your children, you and the mother of your child, you and the relatives of the mother of your child, your children's relationships with your family, etc). All these things should be taken into consideration, because when they are, you usually don't show your ass. Today is eviction day for those people who have taken up too much of my mental and emotional time. Eviction day for those individuals who feel as though they are going to affect my life in ways that force me to act out of character...to you, the space holders..."YOUR LEASE IS UP!" The flip side to this is they're all going to make me rich in the long run. **So on this day, Monday September 13, I say to my former tenants "Thank you...now pack your shit and go!" Keeping it real as always, your girl Kal**

09/14 - The day after the day after the weekend it stormed... and I think I'm going to move. Relocation may just help me sort the givers from the takers and provide the space between us I need to be able to get things in order. Just because you're an author, of which I do not consider myself to be because my books are truth based and not "made up" (to those who read the original When Gucci Came First: true tales of a tramp). So as I was saying, just because you're an author does mean you're Immune to daily drama

And to YOU, Homeboy, I say "Thanks!"

and believe me ... I've got my share. Although it has been quiet today. Thank Goodness...**Love you all -KJ over and OUT!**

09/16 - Haters. Today I want to talk about haters in the "writing community" why? Authors don't hate on me because I'm trying to do my thing. Don't hate on me because I deleted myself from all of your groups, don't be mad because it APPEARS that I may be selling a book or two...I say this after seeing a post re: my book. Now for all y'all who know me you know I'm going to keep it real...this post was classless. called my book INANE PRATTLE, etc. Now that would have offended me HAD I NOT been selling books, that may have offended me HAD I NOT been doing my thing on so many OTHER levels, but fortunate for ME, I AM NOT a hater. I don't have to diss any of you authors, and why should I? and why would I? I've got all y'all books! I have support many of my peers, many authors' books are in my home and I DIDNT GET THEM FOR FREE! The ONLY book I have that I didn't pay for is by someone named Natalie, all the others...RIGHT OUT OF MY POCKET. I was the ONLY author out at the Harlem Book Fair giving out my books for FREE! I was the only author who can honestly say they went around and showed loved to EVERYONE! And in the midst of me being KJ...Not one of them said, "Oh let me buy a book from you kj." But did that stop my flow? Hell no. Did that make me not want to support you? Hell no! So why diss me? If I don't want to send books to be reviewed, don't take it personal, **I TOLD Y'ALL I WAS WRITING, LIVING AND DREAMING**

And to YOU, Homeboy, I say "Thanks!"

FOR THE STREETS, its NOT personal. Kalico Jones is a MOVEMENT, WHERE STREET CREDIBILITY MEETS CORPORATE THINKING. I AM THE BRICK LAYER FOR ALLTHOSE LITTLE KIDS COMING UP WHO ARE IN SITUATIONS WHERE THEY FEEL AS THOUGH THEY CANNOT TURN TO ANYONE. I do many charitable events, I give my time, my money and my spirit for the kids, and don't you even THINK FOR ONE MINUTE YOU CAN JUDGE ME! Please. Now I have better things to do for others, and I cant get them done by allowing the B.S. to get in the way of my goals. Y'all be cool out there. KJ over and OUT! Peace

09/27 - The REAL meaning of keeping it real...and today I'm forced to axe yet another person out of my life. But don't cry for me though, its all good. Now let's get to what I've been up to, my daughter being in a fashion show, dance class, karate, a festival, shopping, dinner, etc. and its been non-stop since Friday afternoon. I've been all over with an authors meeting, a book club meeting and just being a mommy. So between my little princess and my own stuff, it's been one heck of a couple of days. Her fashion debut...well you know how that went down...SHE DID HER THING! she was cute and professional, let me tell you, I may be grooming the next T. Banks. And the dance class, she was terrific! Did you expect anything less than perfection? Of course not! lol. I'm a proud mom. And I should be., it's really all good and I can look and say, **"this is because of me"** and God has my back and

And to YOU, Homeboy, I say "Thanks!"

YOURS too! See ya when I see ya...Kali

                    The 2nd Installment of the Kalico Jones Trilogy

MAN UNNECESSARY
COMING SOON

For all the men who want to know why some women would rather go through life alone than with you.

Meet Edna.

Lets talk about Edna. A project chick with a lot of gusto. Edna loves to live life fast and free. She has no kids, no job, a body that doesn't quit and great facial features, she's a ghetto superstar! You know the saying, "Travel light, travel far!" and that's exactly how Edna lived her life. Every day she kissed the sun as she entered her apartment

And to YOU, Homeboy, I say "Thanks!"

from the night before. Every night finding new faces in crowds where only real players play.

Until…One day after hanging out at the Waterfront Bar & Grill she decides to get in the car with a man she met earlier that night through a friend.

He raped her.
People around the way blamed it on her, saying she should not have taken a ride with someone she didn't know personally, and that may be true in this case, but is it right to blame the victim?

Edna has since become an active voice in her community, speaking out about rape, and offering counseling to women who find themselves victims of this kind of behavior. As of today I can't give you an update, because unfortunately Edna is too busy to talk due to the high volume of victims she sees on a daily basis.

Man Unnecessary!
Lesson here, "No means NO!"

And to YOU, Homeboy, I say "Thanks!"

Karen

Loving, caring, Karen. Grew up the eldest of five and because Karen was the oldest, it was her job to watch her brothers and sisters. Karen resented her mother for forcing her to watch her brothers and sisters, as she was a teen and enjoyed doing teen things. Going to the mall, cheerleading practice, etc. but what could her mother do? Karen's father was not around. And when he was, he was too drunk to care for his own children. He couldn't keep a job and the house payments had to be made. Sometimes there was barely enough money for food, but rest assure in the midst of there not being enough money for food, there was always money for wine and beer.

One payday Karen's mother comes home with bags and bags of groceries for Karen and her siblings. The father walks to the kitchen, shuffles through the bags and yells out to Karen's mother, "Where's my beer?"

"There isn't any."

"What do you mean, there isn't any?"

"There wasn't any money left for me to get your beer."

Karen quickly took the kids into the bedroom, she knew there was going to be fight. Her father always hit her mother when she didn't do as he said. She was scared. But Karen vowed this night would be

And to YOU, Homeboy, I say "Thanks!"

different. She was determined not to let her father beat her mother up tonight. She told her brothers and sisters to stay in their room, gave them the cordless phone and said, "If you hear screaming, call 911, do you understand?" and in unison her siblings said, "Yes." Karen tiptoed into the hall to get a view of her parents. Her father was now standing in front of her mother holding an empty beer bottle and screaming, "There better be some money left to get my fucking beer!" Her mother took a step back and said, "There is no money left, I have no money, the kids need food."

Karen's father grabbed her mother's purse and looked through it throwing papers, her wallet and other contents onto the floor.

"Woman you better go out there and get my fucking beer!" He drew his hand back and slapped Karen's mother to the floor, she let out a scream, "But I have no more money."

"Well then you're gonna get it." He took of his belt and began to hit her. Over and over and over again. Just then Karen runs into the kitchen with a large knife and BOOM!

Karen was too late.

Her mother shot him.

It happened so fast, that her brothers and sisters never got the chance to call 911.

Man Unnecessary!

Stop Domestic Violence. Use your voice, not your fists.

Yelling in the background…

"Tell Kalico not to call here again, we don't want to get involved, whatever is going on between her and homeboy is none of our business, hang up on her ass right now Rich!"

I was on the phone with one of homeboy's cousins, asking him for a number. During our talk, I told him how homeboy hadn't seen his daughter in over one year and was behind in child support. I was only calling to ask for his assistance…to help me help my daughter. We had been in and out of emergency rooms due to what was thought to be Sickle Cell, the doctors needed homeboy's medical history.

I didn't know who else to turn to.

I could not believe Rich's wife, girlfriend or whatever she goes by these days after having just had her third kid by this, another looser in the family…she was yelling, cursing and did she call me a bitch?

Ha…that was easy for her to do, as I was in New Jersey and her ass was in Mt. Vernon. Yeah, I will be that bitch, and maybe homeboy is a looser, but for the most part and other than that…WE – me and my daughter are just fine.

"Richard, why is Adrianne yelling like that in the background? What did I do to her?" as I was utterly confused by her behavior.

"KJ, she does not want you to call here any more. We all know homeboy is fucking up, but there is nothing we can do about it. That's for you two to work out."

"Are you serious? So you're not going to give me his telephone number?"

"No"

"But its Sickle Cell Richard…(took a deep breath) can you please get in contact with him and just give him the number to the hospital? Please?"

(more yelling in the background by Adrianne) "Tell her no…we are

And to YOU, Homeboy, I say "Thanks!"

not getting involved! I told you to hang up!"

I pleaded with Richard to please just pass along the number to homeboy, and as soon as he agreed, his "whatever" got on the phone and said, "Take care of your own business bitch!" and hung up.

WOW, can you believe that shit? This ingrate just hung up on me. She has three children, so it's hard for me to digest the fact that as a mother herself, she showed no compassion for my daughter. Wow.

I called back and let the phone ring. No one picked up.

Good. I will just leave a voice message.

"Hello this is KJ, my apologies for impeding upon your privacy with my issue, clearly this is something that does not involve you, but there is a child in the hospital and this is urgent. I just need to contact homeboy. The doctors are requesting blood work and a possible bone marrow sample from him. They are in need of his family's medical history. We are at Mountainside Hospital in Montclair, NJ should you wish to pass along this message." I left the telephone number to the hospital, my cell number, my job number and my mother's information as well…

I deleted Speedy's cell phone number after that.

And to YOU, Homeboy, I say "Thanks!"

NO ONE got back to us.

NO ONE called the hospital.

I even called homeboy's job.

And …
NOTHING.
Eighteen tests for all sorts of shit and six days later, my daughter was released from the hospital with a clean bill of health.

Thank GOD.

And still not a peep from homeboy.
Notice how I do not capitalize his name. There is no respect there and so I refuse to do it.
So don't worry yourself with that…Just wanted to get that out of the way in the beginning.

At any rate, life goes on.

And to YOU, Homeboy, I say "Thanks!"

Who is MiMi Williamson aka Kalico Jones?

Mimi Williamson is the founder of *The Kalico Jones Project (an online business networking group for African Americans)* and Sole Proprietor of *WildChild Press*, an independent publishing resource for authors who wish to self-publish their works.

She is a resident of East Orange, New Jersey by way of Mt. Vernon, NY where she continues to lend her support. In 2007, *Mimi Williamson* assisted her hometown with it's Mayoral campaign by hosting several online radio interviews with current Mayor Mr. Clinton Young and former Mayor Mr. Ernest Davis, which was one of the closest Mayoral races in Mt. Vernon history, and by far the most controversial.

Her grass roots approach to rally young voters was recognized and applauded by both current Mayor Mr. Clinton Young and former Mayor Mr. Ernest Davis.

As a young lady who grew up in an environment that was abusive. *Mimi Williamson,* made a conscious decision to not only pen her

And to YOU, Homeboy, I say "Thanks!"

life story under the brand, *"Kalico Jones"* but to actively work to assist young people in their quest to become successes in their own right. She prides herself on her determination to "Beat the odds" by focusing on her education and natural talents.

Although her titles (five books and counting…) are not for audiences under 18, *Mimi Williamson's* life experiences give her added value at what she does. Physically abused, sexually abused, emotionally abused, drugs, being kicked out of school at 16, *Mimi Williamson* appeared to be a statistic.

But despite being told she would never amount to anything, *Mimi Williamson* turned her life around. She set realistic goals for herself and achieved them one by one. At 19 she graduated from Monroe College in New Rochelle, NY and by the time she was 21, she was working at a leading Wall Street firm. She then went on to secure positions within National Geographic Magazine, Deloitte & Touché and WorldCom, all leading companies in their respective fields at the time.

During her "time" in Corporate America, *Mimi Williamson* realized her true passion; to work with "at risk" teens and women / families in transitional stages, and so I introduce to you…*Mimi Williamson* AND *The Kalico Jones project.*

COMMUNITY INITIATIVES UNDER THE KJP:

CROSS OUR T'S

 The 2nd Installment of the Kalico Jones Trilogy

And to YOU, Homeboy, I say "Thanks!"

Cross Our Ts was created by Mimi Williamson, who has taken a personal interest in promoting the importance of education, self respect, and health & well being to teens, including HIV/AIDS prevention, through interactive teen friendly seminars.

"Cross Our T's offers teens REAL life solutions in an open dialogue to REAL life issues and concerns."

KJ CARES

A community based organization that believes in grassroots approaches to community challenges. Fund Raising initiatives. Voter registration drives. Food / Clothing drives. A true effort to immobilize the surrounding community leaders / business owners, residents to GIVE BACK!

The KALICO JONES Project

Black2Black Business Networking

Mission: To provide a networking resource that expands the possibilities of initial ideas, and concepts according to the "each one teach one" methodology for the African American Community.

"By sharing information we allow our efforts to be supported and developed through the experiences and assistance of others."

KJ's KIDS

For Kids, about Kids, KJ loves the kids!

Events / Book Clubs / Scholarships and more!

The 2nd Installment of the Kalico Jones Trilogy 171

And to YOU, Homeboy, I say "Thanks!"

For speaking engagements please call 973-672-2753

Email: kalicojones@yahoo.com

Website: www.thekalicojonesproject.com

"The Cross Our T's" initiative & The Kalico Jones Project is a wonderful program headed by a person who in all rights is a hero herself."